SUMMER'S DREAM

Talented designer Juliet Croft is devastated when the company she works for closes. She takes a temporary job at the Linden Manor Hotel, but soon hears rumours that the business is in financial difficulties — and suspects that Sheldon's, a rival company, is involved. During her work, she renews her friendship with Scott, a former colleague. At the same time, she must cope with her growing feelings for Martin Glover, the hotel manager. Trouble is, he's already taken . . .

JEAN M. LONG

SUMMER'S DREAM

Complete and Unabridged

LINFORD
Leicester

First published in Great Britain in 2017

First Linford Edition
published 2017

A catalogue record for this book is available
from the British Library.

ISBN 978–1–4448–3185–6

Published by
F. A. Thorpe (Publishing)
Anstey, Leicestershire

Set by Words & Graphics Ltd.
Anstey, Leicestershire
Printed and bound in Great Britain by
T. J. International Ltd., Padstow, Cornwall

This book is printed on acid-free paper

1

Juliet leant back on the sun-lounger and gave a contented sigh. Marina's small garden was a blaze of colour, and beyond was an idyllic view over the Weald of Kent. This was just what she needed after the past few months. She stretched lazily. The prospect of three or four weeks here was wonderful.

She'd just completed a final commission for Cramphorn's — the interior design company she'd been employed by — and now she was having to think hard about what she was going to do next.

Right out of the blue her boss, Duncan Cramphorn, had announced he was winding up the business and then, to her utter astonishment, had proposed to her.

'I'm off to Somerset, Juliet, and I'd love you to come with me — as my wife,' he'd told her.

She'd been flattered and touched by

his proposal but, although fond of him, Juliet had absolutely no romantic feelings for him whatsoever, so she'd declined. Even now, she could see the disappointment etched on his kindly face. If she'd accepted, it would certainly have solved a great many problems, but it would have created another set. For a start, he was practically old enough to be her father!

She closed her eyes and opened them again abruptly as her mobile rang. She snatched it up.

'Hi, Juliet — Karen here.'

'Karen! How are things?'

'Couldn't be better. The new job's just what I wanted. I've really fallen on my feet. How're you?'

Duncan's former PA remained a good friend of Juliet's, even though they hadn't met up for a while. They chatted for a few minutes, and then Karen said, 'I didn't realise you were on holiday. I was ringing to let you know about a Homes and Gardens Fayre that's on next week. Sounds interesting. Thought it might be useful if you're still proposing to go freelance on your interior design.'

'Oh — I'm not sure. I've just finished that last big commission and I could actually do with a bit of time to chill out and relax. Seems like I've been working flat out for months! So where's this Fayre being held?'

There was a slight pause. 'Linden Manor Hotel.'

'Linden Manor!' Juliet echoed. 'But that was the place … '

'Yes, I know. Sheldon Enterprises did its makeover — but Juliet, that was almost three years ago. It's all in the past now; time to move on. Besides, Elizabeth Sheldon's living in America now.'

Juliet swallowed. 'Right.'

There was another pause and then Karen said casually, 'I've got a spare ticket, if you're interested.'

Juliet considered. What had she got to lose?

'OK, thanks. It'll be great to see you again. Actually, I'm staying in Kent with Marina Norris. You remember, the lady I used to lodge with when I first worked for Cramphorn's.'

'Yes, of course — I remember Marina well. She only retired a short while back, didn't she? Her needlework skills are awesome.'

'Too true! She's really talented. You should see some of the beautiful stuff she's got in this place. I've got the most unbelievable patchwork quilt on my bed here.'

They chatted away for a little longer. It was good to catch up on all the news. No sooner had Juliet put her mobile away than Marina appeared carrying a laden tea-tray. 'I saw you were on the phone — is everything OK, dear?'

Juliet nodded. 'Yes, I've just had an unexpected invitation. A friend I worked with at Cramphorn's has invited me to a Homes and Gardens Fayre at Linden Manor Hotel.'

Marina raised her eyebrows. 'That's a very upmarket place these days, so I've heard. I'd give my eye teeth to take a look round.'

'I could probably wangle you an invite

too. It's next Tuesday.'

Marina looked disappointed. 'That's kind, dear, but something's cropped up which I need to talk to you about. Anyway, first of all, tell me what's bothering you — I can see something is — and then I'll tell you about my predicament.'

As they sat over cups of tea and slices of Victoria sandwich, Juliet began to relax.

'Sheldon's — the firm that did up Linden Manor — caused most of the problem for Cramphorn's. I'm convinced that was partly why Duncan decided to wind up the business.'

'Mmm. Refresh my memory, dear.'

'Sheldon's had always been a rival to Cramphorn's, but when the daughter, Elizabeth Sheldon, started working there, she really stirred things up. Somehow, she was finding out about the contracts Duncan was about to secure, contacting the people involved and making them a cheaper offer.

'Not only that. Somehow our designs were stolen and copied, particularly the soft furnishings that Elizabeth Sheldon was responsible for. Duncan suspected one of our designers, Evan Dean, although we couldn't prove anything.'

'Yes, I heard about that,' Marina said gently and Juliet lowered her gaze. The memories were just too painful. She'd been in a relationship with Evan at that time had been sure that he was the one for her. She'd been contemplating wedding bells when she discovered that he was having an affair … with Elizabeth Sheldon.

'There was a show-down,' she murmured. 'It was dreadful. There was no proof. Evan stormed off, leaving us to sort out the mess. Unfortunately, the business seemed to be on a downward spiral after that.'

There was a silence. Marina stirred her tea. 'So what are you planning to do now?'

'I'm thinking of going freelance. I've done a bit from time to time, when things at Cramphorn's were a bit slack. Anyway, what's your predicament? Nothing serious, I hope.'

Marina's kindly face looked worried. 'Not exactly — but I've done something so stupid you just wouldn't credit it!'

Juliet helped herself to a scone and spread it liberally with butter and jam. 'I'm sure it can't be that bad. I honestly don't believe you're capable of anything stupid.'

'You will when I tell you. I've double booked myself! Some friends and I arranged to go on holiday ages ago. I honestly thought it was next month, but I must have turned two pages over when I marked it on the calendar — turns out, it's next week.'

Juliet tried to conceal her disappointment. 'Oh, well never mind. I'll go home. I can always come to visit another time when it's more convenient.'

'Oh, no, Juliet, you must stay. I wouldn't dream of cutting your holiday short. Besides, I was hoping you'd look after Smudge. She's getting elderly now and I wouldn't want to have to put her in a cattery. She wouldn't like it, would you, Smudge?'

Hearing her name, Smudge appeared by Marina's side and nuzzled the pocket where her mistress kept her treats.

'Well — if you're sure.'

It wasn't how Juliet had envisaged spending her holiday. She hadn't seen her friend Marina for a couple of years and it had seemed like a good opportunity to catch up with each other and explore Kent, a county she didn't know too well.

'I'm afraid that's not all,' Marina said after a few moments. 'It's actually possible I might have treble booked!'

Juliet stared at her, wondering what was coming next.

'I'd better explain. My brother and I own this house jointly. It was left to us by our parents. Edward was already married with his own home, so he's always allowed me to live here, on condition that if he or any of the family want to stay when they're in the area, they could do so — handy to London, you see.'

Juliet nodded, trying to make sense of this.

Marina set Smudge on the grass. 'It's

Edward's sister-in-law's sixtieth birthday and there's to be a party whilst I'm away. There's a distinct possibility one or the other of the family might want to stay here for a day or two.'

Juliet swallowed. 'That's OK,' she said brightly. 'Unless they're likely to mind that I'm staying here?'

Marina looked awkward. 'Of course not, dear. There's plenty of space. Anyway, the chances are they won't even want to come here. Actually, you know Edward's son — my nephew, Scott — don't you? He used to work at Cramphorn's.'

'Oh yes. I'd forgotten you were related. I always got on well with Scott, but I lost track of him when he left.'

Marina ran her fingers through her iron grey hair. 'It's just come to me as we've been talking about Linden Manor Hotel. I'm sure that's where he's working now. Why on earth didn't I remember before?'

Juliet was taken aback. Scott was a thoroughly nice guy, and she'd enjoyed working with him. Surely Karen would have mentioned it if she'd known he'd been working at Linden Manor?

'Really! It's a small world,' she said lightly, and thought Marina seemed relieved.

The older woman picked up the plate of scones and passed it to her. 'It certainly is. Now, how about another scone?'

★　★　★

Linden Manor Hotel was even more elegant than Juliet remembered it. She had to concede that Elizabeth Sheldon had made a good job of things, even if she had copied other people's designs. It was certainly swish; Juliet's feet sank into the soft pile of the dove-grey carpet, which toned with the pale pink walls and deeper pink curtains. It was a shame Marina couldn't have come. The older woman would have loved it, but she was busy with last-minute holiday matters.

Juliet gazed about her. She just needed to locate the ballroom where Karen had arranged to meet up with her. As she crossed the large reception area a tall, fair-haired man came down the stairs two at a time, and stopped in front of her stretching out a hand.

'Welcome. I'm Martin Glover, the manager here. Your interview is taking place in my office if you'd care to follow me. We've got a Homes and Gardens Fayre on today, so it's a bit manic.'

And he shot off before Juliet could point out his mistake. She was itching to see more of the hotel and, on an impulse, followed him up the oak staircase, along a corridor, and into an office which seemed more like a library, with its book-lined walls.

He indicated a chair and picked up an impressive-looking CV. He studied it for a moment or two and Juliet studied him, noting the thick, fair hair framing his lean features and the slight dimple in his chin.

'Before we begin, would you like a coffee?'

Juliet declined and pushed back a strand of dark hair nervously. She knew she ought to come clean but wondered just how long she could keep this charade

up. Just then the phone rang. She realised, from the conversation, that he was
speaking to the actual candidate. He put
down the phone with a bang and turned
to her with a face like a thundercloud.

'So if you're not Miss Barlow then who
on earth are you? Oh, let me guess, you're
a journalist taking the opportunity to
snoop about.'

Now why hadn't she thought of that?
'You just didn't give me a chance to explain. I'm actually here for the Fayre.'

His eyebrows shot up. He got to his
feet. 'I see. So may I see your ticket? We
can't be too careful these days. Have to
watch out for gate-crashers. This is quite
a prestigious event.'

Juliet felt the colour rising her cheeks.
'My friend's holding my ticket for me. Do
I look like a gate-crasher?' she demanded
indignantly.

He looked her up and down. 'Well, you
don't have any dark glasses and I don't
think you're wearing a wig — but didn't
you see the signs and arrows? The back
of the hotel is available for the Fayre,

and we're endeavouring to keep the front reserved for guests who are staying here, and for the interviews.'

'Right. Sounds a bit like *Upstairs, Downstairs*, to me,' Juliet told him, and made a hasty exit before he could think of a suitable rejoinder.

She eventually located the ballroom and found Karen looking out for her from a stand just inside the door. She laughed when Juliet told her about her recent encounter with Martin Glover.

'He's very nice really, when you get to know him.'

'I'll take your word for it. You've obviously met him before then?'

Karen hesitated fractionally. 'Yes, our paths have crossed. Come on, let's take a look round. Actually, I am supposed to be on duty today, so I might have to leave you to your own devices for a bit, but I'm all right for a few minutes.'

Juliet looked at her in surprise. 'Oh, I hadn't realised. I thought it was your day off. So has your firm got a stand here?'

Karen hesitated again. 'Not exactly.

Look, I'd better give you your ticket — just in case you run into Martin Glover again.'

Juliet felt that Karen wasn't too keen to say much about her job, and wondered why. After a while, her friend excused herself, promising they'd meet up later for coffee.

Juliet went outside. Linden Manor was just as impressive from the back. She stood for a moment, admiring the magnificent red-brick house. It was enjoyable wandering round the stalls in the sunshine, and she began to relax.

She examined the work samples on several of the stands, thumbed through albums of photographs and read a number of recommendations from satisfied customers. She decided that her standard of work equalled what she could see displayed here.

'Juliet! Karen said you were coming today!'

The dark-haired young man enveloped her in a bear hug, planting a kiss on her cheek.

Juliet beamed at him. 'Scott! How lovely to see you! I'm staying with your Aunt Marina.'

'Yes, I know. I spoke to her on the phone a few days ago. It's great to see you, Juliet. It's been too long since we last met up.'

Juliet nodded. Scott was an amiable young man, very much like Marina. His hair was shorter than when she'd last seen him, and he was wearing an expensive-looking jacket with a crisp, open-necked shirt beneath, and dark trousers.

'I didn't realise you were working here, Scott.'

'Yes, I've been here for around eight months now. I'm the assistant manager. We must get together sometime for a drink, Juliet. There just never seem to be enough hours in the day, though!'

'Well when you find a window let me know. I'd love to meet up. I'm probably going to be around for the next three or four weeks. After that — who knows?'

Refreshments were being served at one end of the ballroom and Juliet went off for a coffee and to peruse the sheaf of papers she'd accumulated. Glancing round the room, she spotted Karen talking to Martin Glover.

From where Juliet was sitting she had a good view of him. He was immaculately attired, and she supposed he was quite good-looking. He could obviously turn on the charm when it suited him.

A moment or two later Martin came across to her table.

'Hallo again.' He squatted on the edge of a chair. 'I've just been speaking to Karen — didn't realise the pair of you had worked together at Cramphorn's. You should have said.'

Juliet raised her eyebrows. 'Why? Would it have made any difference?'

He grinned. 'Look, I realise how I must have come across earlier but, in my defence, we're very short-staffed at present and these past couple of days I've been run ragged.'

'Poor you!' she said with a touch of sarcasm which surprised even herself.

He got to his feet. 'Well now, if you

don't want my apology there's not much I can do, is there?'

The slightest hint of a smile touched her mouth. 'OK, so what's the vacancy for, anyway?' she asked curiously.

'Reception. Although, initially, it's more for a general factotum — providing cover where and when it's needed.'

He sat down again. 'Might you be interested? Karen said you were looking for work.'

'Yes, I am although … ' She frowned, wondering why on earth Karen thought she'd be interested in being a receptionist. She didn't finish her sentence, but instead asked another question. 'So — how come you know Karen?'

His eyes widened. 'Didn't she say? She's my PA.'

Juliet stared at him. 'Karen is your PA,' she repeated slowly. 'I'd no idea.'

He looked amused. 'It's very different from Cramphorn's but, as you can see, there's plenty going on to keep her occupied. It's the best venue in the area for events like this one. It's got the most suitable grounds and amenities.'

'Yes, I see,' she said inanely, although she didn't really see at all. She'd not questioned where Karen was working and now realised her friend had been economical with the truth.

She looked in Karen's direction, hoping to catch her attention, but she was deep in conversation with an elderly lady wearing a shocking-pink hat.

Martin excused himself and, a moment or two later, Karen came to join her, carrying a cup of coffee.

'Phew it's busy — not that I'm complaining. I'm taking a breather for a few minutes. I saw you were talking to Martin. What's up — didn't it go well?'

'Karen, why didn't you tell me you were working here as Martin's PA?'

Karen looked surprised. 'Didn't I say? Must have assumed you knew.'

The day had taken on a different dimension.

'Did you know there might be some work available when you contacted me?' Juliet demanded.

'Not exactly. The girl who's got the job at the moment isn't leaving for another couple of weeks. She and her husband are off abroad. We need to get things sorted ASAP, but we've only had three applicants who were anything like suitable.'

She sat down. 'The first one was offered another job a couple of days ago. Applicant number two was completely unsuitable and, as you know, the third candidate pulled out this morning.'

'OK — so what exactly did you tell Martin Glover? He obviously thinks I was in an admin job like you. Does he actually know what I've been doing?'

Karen toyed with her coffee cup. 'No, although, he's obviously aware Cramphorn's was an interior design company ... Juliet, you've got oodles of experience of dealing upfront with customers. Go on — it'd be a laugh.'

'I'm not sure I get the joke, Karen. I came to Kent for a holiday whilst I was thinking out what I wanted to do with my life.'

Karen said persuasively, 'This'd be a

doddle in comparison with what you've been used to doing *and* it's part-time. I've heard a rumour that the owners might soon be thinking of doing up some more rooms on the second floor. So, there might well be some interior design work here for you. You could always put in a quote. This place is definitely on the map, and it's expanding!'

There was something Juliet needed to know. 'So what became of Sheldon Interiors?'

Karen shrugged. 'Not sure. Rather think it's moved abroad. That last little fiasco put the kibosh on it.'

They chatted on for a bit and then Karen said, 'Come and meet some of the other members of our team.'

Karen introduced her to three other members of the hotel staff — Iain Mason, Layla Hicks and Adam Judd. Shortly afterwards, Scott came across to join them. They were a friendly crowd, and it wasn't long before Juliet was thinking a change of scenery and a less pressurised job might very well suit her for a few months. It would give her some breathing space — just until she'd got herself sorted out with a business plan for the bank.

As she prepared to leave, she saw Martin Glover deep in conversation with Scott. Glancing in her direction, Scott murmured something to Martin, who shook his head. Juliet felt uncomfortably aware that they were discussing her.

Scott caught up with her in the car park. 'Juliet, I meant what I said. I'd really like to see you again so that we can have a proper chat. I've just had a thought. I've been invited to my Aunt's sixtieth birthday party, but it would be so much better if I had someone to go with. Would you consider being my partner for the evening?'

Juliet smiled at Scott. He was such a nice, uncomplicated sort of guy. Periodically, after she'd split up with Evan, she'd accompanied Scott to functions connected with work, but not to anything like this party.

'I'd like that, Scott. So, do I take it things didn't work out between you and Kelly?'

He grinned. 'Kelly was great, but she was just out for a good time. I'm looking for a relationship that's a bit more permanent.'

'Oh, you'll find the right girl eventually,' she said and put a hand on his arm just as Martin Glover walked past. Now he would get totally the wrong impression. Although why on earth would that matter? she wondered. She'd only just met him and he could think what he liked. What was it to her?

That evening, Scott's parents rang to say they'd like to stay with Marina for a few days. The following morning Marina and Juliet did a big supermarket shop and restocked the freezer, and then they made up the bed in the largest guest room.

On Thursday, Juliet took Marina into Canterbury to do some necessary last -minute shopping for her holiday. Marina confessed she hated looking for new clothes, and would value Juliet's opinion. They had a fun time and emerged from the department stores laden with carrier bags. Juliet had treated herself to a new dress for Saturday's party.

'Come on, it's getting frantically busy — full of tourists. Let's go and have a quiet lunch. I know the very place. It's only a short detour on our way home.'

The pub Marina recommended was in an attractive setting by the river. They opted to sit outside and Juliet went to the bar to order. To her astonishment she found herself standing next to Martin Glover.

'Hello there. We meet again.'

He was served with his drinks and waited whilst she collected hers and gave her food order. He walked with her to her table and Juliet had no alternative but to introduce him to Marina. Marina smiled and then looked at him, head on one side.

'Haven't we met before? I feel as if I should know you from somewhere.'

Martin looked startled and shook his head. 'I'm sorry, I don't remember — unless you've been to Linden Manor Hotel?'

'Not since it became so upmarket, no,' she said, and Juliet got the distinct impression that Martin was looking uncomfortable. He glanced around him as if anxious to make his escape.

Just then a petite blonde woman stood up, waved her hands and called, 'Over here, Martin.'

He smiled at the pair of them and moved off.

'That was strange,' Marina said. 'For a moment it felt as if a ghost was walking over my grave. It was the oddest sensation, but I really felt I knew that young man.'

Juliet looked across at the table where he sat chatting to his companion.

'She's very pretty, isn't she?'

Marina gave her a surprised look. 'Nothing out of the ordinary. That dress must have cost a small fortune. So, would you consider working at the hotel if you got the opportunity?'

Juliet thought for a moment. 'It would be a complete change, and it would give me the chance to sort myself out without having to worry about spending all my savings. Although, I'm not at all sure there really is an opening for me. I get the distinct impression Martin Glover would be quite a difficult man to please.'

Marina glanced across at the couple, a slight frown on her face. 'You've got to sell yourself, Juliet. I know your worth. You're a very talented young woman. If you want that job then go for it, my girl!'

Juliet smiled at the older woman. 'All right, you've convinced me. I will!'

★ ★ ★

David and Iris Norris turned out to be a delightful couple who insisted on taking Marina and Juliet out to lunch when they arrived on Friday.

Marina left early on Saturday morning. Scott's parents and Juliet had a leisurely day before the party that evening.

Juliet was relieved that she'd brought the dress. It was an electric blue shift, and she teamed it with black, patent-leather sandals. She swept her gleaming brown hair to the top of her head, in what she hoped was a sophisticated style, applied some light make-up, gathered up her shrug, and went downstairs.

'Wow!' Scott said approvingly. 'I'm more used to seeing you in jeans. You look fantastic, Juliet!'

They drove round narrow country lanes and suddenly the landscape seemed familiar.

'Where is your aunt's birthday party, Scott? I completely forgot to ask.'

'It's at Linden Manor — staff discount. Can't believe no-one's told you,' he said incredulously.

Juliet swallowed. 'Twice in one week. How's that for a coincidence!'

She couldn't seem to keep away from the place. An image of Martin Glover sprang into her mind. Would he be on duty tonight? She wondered if the relationship between him and the beautiful leggy blonde was serious. Juliet dismissed the thought. Why ever would it matter to her?

A few minutes later they swung through the gateway of Linden Manor and along the tree-lined drive. Scott's parents were already there, talking with his Uncle Paul and his wife, Rhoda, who greeted them warmly. Juliet was relieved she'd managed to get her a small gift.

The meal was a delight and Juliet found the company interesting. Afterwards, they were invited to go into the ballroom where a band was playing. Coffee was served and the party took off with a swing.

Much to Juliet's amusement, she soon discovered that Scott was not into the more traditional type of dancing and created steps of his own to fit the music. He seemed tireless and eventually, pleading for mercy, she sank thankfully onto the nearest chair. It was hot in the room and she longed to escape out into the invitingly cool-looking garden.

Scott was doing his best to persuade her back onto the dance floor when she saw someone beckoning to him from the far door. With bad grace, he went across to find out what was wrong. After a few moments, when he didn't return, Juliet went to join him.

'One of the bar staff has rung in sick.

We're short-staffed as it is. Juliet I'm so sorry but I'll have to cover until we can sort something out.'

'Not to worry, I'll join you. It's very hot in there anyway.'

'That's another thing. I bet the air conditioning is on the blink again.'

Scott made his excuses to his family and, catching Juliet by the hand, led her out into the entrance hall and into the bar where a handful of guests was sitting.

A few minutes later he had donned a different jacket, and was expertly serving drinks. Juliet watched in some surprise, wondering where he'd learnt this skill. He seemed to be able to keep up the banter whilst mixing cocktails.

After a while she decided it wasn't her scene, and told Scott she was going for a walk. It was still quite light outside, and there were solar lights at the edge of the path. She inhaled the scent from the roses and lavender in the deep flower borders. More and more, it became apparent that this could be a pleasant place to work whilst she was gathering her ideas together for her future career.

Deep in thought, she was suddenly confronted by a brick wall and, seeing a door marked *Private Staff Only*, felt a bit like Alice in Wonderland as she pushed it open.

Finding herself in an attractive little garden with a fountain in its midst, she drew a deep breath of pure pleasure. She wandered round, enchanted, until suddenly she came upon a small rose arbour. She was about to sit down when a figure suddenly loomed at her. She stifled a scream as she realised it was Martin Glover.

'Miss Croft, we meet again! Are you lost or just determined to trespass?'

2

Blushing furiously, Juliet sank onto the seat. 'I'm with Scott Norris at his aunt's party.'

'Do you know all my staff?'

'Only the ones who worked for Cramphorn's.'

'Right. So where is Scott?'

'Helping out in the bar.'

'Scott's working? He's supposed to be off duty tonight.'

'Apparently you're short-staffed.'

'Oh. So he's sent you to find me?'

She shook her head. 'It was hot in the ballroom so I decided to come for a walk to cool down. I hadn't a clue where you were.'

She realised that the close proximity of this man was unnerving her. She caught a waft of his spicy cologne.

'Right. I'd better get back, I suppose.' He sighed. 'No rest for the wicked! Tell me, how did you get in here?'

'Through the door in the wall.'

'Someone's left it open again.' Standing up, he pulled some keys from his pocket. 'If you wait whilst I lock that door, I'll walk back with you. It was thoughtful of Scott to let me have my break, but it's practically finished.'

He held out his hand and helped her to her feet, and she caught her breath at the touch of his fingers. This man was seriously attractive. She felt a slight stab of guilt as she remembered she was here with Scott.

'Karen tells me you might be interested in joining our team.'

'I, er …' Juliet stammered.

'If you're serious, you can present for interview next Tuesday at eleven o'clock,' he told her without preamble.

'I'd need to see a job description,' she told him reasonably.

'Absolutely — ask Karen. She'll find you one. And I, in turn, will naturally need to see your CV. I think you've been used to doing something rather different from what we're wanting here.'

She hesitated. 'I'll be frank, Mr Glover. I wouldn't want to waste my time applying for this job, only to be told that you've considered me to be an unsuitable candidate from the outset.'

She thought she detected a slight smile at the corner of his mouth.

'And I would hope you wouldn't waste my time by applying for a job if you weren't prepared to be totally committed.'

They continued to walk back to the hotel in silence. He took her by a short cut through a small copse, and then in through a side door. She followed him to the bar where Scott was in deep conversation with the leggy blonde Martin had been with in the pub in Canterbury.

'There you are, Martin. We nearly sent out a search party!' She gave Juliet a cool stare.

'I've told you I'm on duty tonight, Amanda,' he said rather dismissively. 'Scott, I'm here now, so you must return to the party and take Miss ... er, Juliet with you. She got rather lost in the grounds.'

Scott's mother was looking worried as they re-entered the ballroom. 'I'd no idea you'd be gone that long. It's the best part of an hour. You should put your foot down about working when it's supposed to be your evening off.'

'I'm the assistant manager, Mum, and it was an emergency. Anyway, it's all sorted now. Martin's taken over from me, so there's no problem.'

'For a hotel like this, it seems to be a bit disorganised,' his mother remarked. 'Fortunately, Rhoda's having the time of her life.'

Juliet wished she was outside again, walking alongside Martin Glover. His fingers had touched hers like a gentle caress. She knew nothing about him but he had already made a lasting impression on her.

★　★　★

Karen leant back on the garden seat and sipped her cool drink. 'Oh, this is the life for me. Pity I'm back on duty again this afternoon.'

33

'So tell me, Karen, how come you applied for the job at Linden Manor?' Juliet asked.

'Iain. I've known him for years. His parents own the adjoining holiday cottage to this one, and my family and his often met up during the summer. Anyway, he got a job at Linden Manor first and then, when he told me about it, I decided to have a go.

'I started off doing general admin, but when Martin's PA left I decided to apply. My parents are happy for me to live in their holiday cottage, and Iain and I have become — well, close. Things couldn't have worked out better for me.'

'That's great. I'm really made up for you.'

Karen plumped up the cushion and settled herself more comfortably. 'And, what about your family? Didn't you tell me your parents have moved?'

'Yes, they've gone to be nearer my sister, Sarah, in Wiltshire. They love every minute of it, and they're in their element helping out with Sarah's little twins.'

'So now that you've severed your links with Hertfordshire, are you going to apply for that job?'

Juliet picked up her glass. 'I suppose I could give it a go. You'll need to fill me in on a few things first though.'

'Martin will want to see an up to the minute CV.'

'No problem. I've brought my file with me, just in case. And I've got my laptop for my letter. I can print it in the library. I've looked at the form and it's quite straightforward.'

'It is, really. It's mainly reception, but when we're short-staffed you could be asked to take on a variety of different roles.'

Karen outlined the sort of work Juliet might find herself faced with. It couldn't have been more different from what she'd been used to doing at Cramphorn's.

'So what d'you think?' Karen asked.

'I'm prepared to give it a go. What you may not know, my friend, is that yours truly did a stint in a hotel when I was at uni — so I'm not totally without experience.'

'Right. So, you'd be asked to shadow for a few days and, until you've had your references checked and so on, you'll probably find yourself behind the scenes — helping in the kitchen or doing something boring like photocopying.'

'Are you trying to put me off? Have you had second thoughts?'

'As if!' Karen protested. 'It'll be great fun. You'll see. Would you be able to carry on staying with Marina? I'd offer you to share with me, but there are only two bedrooms and my parents might want to stay.'

Juliet stared at her friend. 'I'd somehow assumed there'd be a room for me at the hotel. It's a bit isolated. I'm not sure I could impose on Marina for too long and I certainly couldn't commute from Hertfordshire.'

Karen hesitated. 'The thing is, the staff quarters are pretty awful. Personally, I think that's why Martin finds it so difficult to keep staff.'

Juliet was taken aback. 'How d'you mean? Does he expect us to camp in the grounds or something?'

Karen laughed. 'No, it's just that — oh, you'll see for yourself. The contrast is unbelievable. There are those wonderful rooms on the ground floor; the reception area, restaurant, ballroom, visitors' lounge and several lovely bedrooms. On the first floor is the bridal suite and a few more bedrooms, all beautifully appointed, but that's it.'

Juliet frowned. 'How d'you mean — *that's it?* I've seen Martin Glover's office. I'll admit it wasn't exactly state of the art, but it was adequate, so what exactly are you saying?'

Karen cupped her hands behind her head. 'There are lots of other rooms, but they're not being used because they aren't in any fit condition to be given to visitors.'

Juliet stared at her friend. 'So, are you telling me that there might be some work for me in the interior design field, or what?'

Karen shrugged. 'It's all a bit mysterious. I really believed so up until recently, because we've had to turn people away — send them to other hotels due to lack of decent accommodation here.'

Juliet's heart sank. 'You're not painting me a very good picture, Karen.'

Karen sighed. 'Yes, I know and I'm sorry. You see, up until about a week ago, I really thought Linden Manor Hotel was on the map. But then — Juliet, this is in the strictest confidence — Iain overheard Martin on the phone. It wasn't intentional — the door was open. Martin seemed to be having a conversation with one of the owners, and it was all very negative from what Iain made out.'

Juliet sat up. 'Go on,' she urged.

'Martin was obviously talking about expansion, but whoever he was speaking to was having none of it. Martin was in a bad mood for the rest of the day.'

'So, who exactly are the owners? Will they be at my interview?'

Karen shook her head. 'None of us has ever met them. Martin says they live some distance away. He seems to be given a fairly free hand when it comes to making decisions about the day to day running of the place, but obviously the owners control the purse strings.'

'Right. Thanks for sharing this, Karen. It certainly puts a different complexion on things. You've put me in two minds as to whether I should go ahead with this interview. After all, I've just recently departed one sinking ship!'

Karen was silent for a moment or two. 'I wouldn't blame you if you backed out, but who knows? Being the perpetual optimist, things might suddenly look up. Linden Manor really is a lovely place to work. There's a happy atmosphere and the staff are a great crowd — as you've seen for yourself. And there could be such a lot of scope for your interior design skills. It's only an idea, but I wondered — supposing we went all out to do up one of the rooms for your use? Give it the wow factor! It would give Martin an idea of what you were capable of doing. Then he might be able to persuade the owners to let you refurbish a couple more guest rooms.'

'Or we could buy a fistful of lottery tickets and if we won, blow it on refurbishing the place, I suppose.'

Karen gave her a withering look. 'Come on, Juliet. I believe in Linden Manor, and if you came on board, I'm sure you would too.'

'We're back to ships again,' Juliet said and they both laughed. 'OK, I'll give it a trial run. After all, nothing else has cropped up, and I could prepare a book of recommendations whilst I'm doing whatever I'm asked to do.'

'I'll get us some lunch and then we'll do a mock interview. We're going to have fun, Juliet!'

Juliet smiled and wondered what she was letting herself in for, but she knew she'd enjoy getting to know more about Martin Glover.

⋆   ⋆   ⋆

The interview went better than Juliet could ever have hoped for. There was one tricky moment when Martin Glover asked her what she thought she could bring to Linden Manor Hotel.

'I have had plenty of experience of

40

dealing with members of the public, and I've worked in an hotel during my Uni vacs,' she told him.

'Mmm but, looking at your CV, that must have been some eight or nine years ago.'

Juliet nodded. 'Yes, I appreciate I'd need to brush up on my skills. As I've explained, my main focus in recent years has been on interior design.'

Martin gave her a searching glance from dark-green eyes, the colour of Cornish serpentine stone, she decided.

'Well I can't guarantee there'd be an opening for you here in that field. It isn't what we're looking for at the moment, although you'd be welcome to refurbish your own room — that's if you wanted to be resident.'

He leant forward on his chair and gave her a searching glance. 'Tell me, Juliet, were you involved in that business with Sheldon Enterprises?'

She looked at him, startled. 'Actually, yes. I was working at Cramphorn's and the contract was to have gone to them

…' She trailed off as a flood of memories washed over her. 'It's something I'd rather not dwell on — if you don't mind.'

Martin nodded. 'OK. So, to get back to my previous question. Apart from interior design, what else could you bring to Linden Manor Hotel?'

'I'm enthusiastic and reliable,' she said earnestly. 'You could expect loyalty and total commitment.'

She could see that he was waiting for her to say something else, and added simply, 'As an interior designer, I'm expected to show a fresh approach to things and that's what I would do here.'

He nodded and seemed satisfied. 'Now, as I'm sure you'll appreciate, we can't have you working front of house until we've checked your references. But you *can* shadow Layla on the desk. When a suitable course arises, I'll send you on it. In the meantime, as I've explained, you might be asked to lend a hand wherever needed. If that would suit you, then you could start next Monday.'

After a few more minutes, he took Juliet

to see the staff accommodation. They stood in the doorway of a large room on the third floor. As Karen had warned her, it was extremely basic. But she caught a glimpse of an en suite, so at least she wouldn't have to share a bathroom.

'You would be free to try your hand at refurbishing this. I can't offer you much — say, a hundred pounds.'

It would cost far more than that, but Juliet liked a challenge. She suddenly caught sight of the superb view from the window, which was a selling point in itself. She smiled. 'I'll certainly have my work cut out, but I'd like to give it a go.'

Martin looked relieved. 'Good. I'm afraid we haven't been able to do up as many rooms as I would have liked. Now, it's a lovely day so let's go outside and have some coffee.'

They sat on the veranda facing the grounds and Juliet realised that she would enjoy working in these idyllic surroundings, just as Karen had predicted. A young girl brought a tray of coffee and Martin Glover poured it into delicate china cups.

Over coffee he asked if she had any further questions.

'Am I right in thinking not too many of the staff live in?' she ventured.

He nodded. 'Enough to cover emergencies. Scott and I do for a start, but Karen, Iain and Layla all live out. Some of the catering and bar staff have rooms here.'

'So when I'm off duty, should I wish to stay around here, what would there be for me to do?'

'Oh, I didn't show you the staff sitting-room. Again, it's rather basic, but there's the usual TV and, in the basement, table tennis. You're entitled to swim in the pool and use the tennis courts — if they're not in great demand. The nearest village, where Karen and Iain live, is a couple of miles away.'

Shortly afterwards, Martin got to his feet. 'Duty calls. We'll give it a trial run — shall we say a month on either side?'

She smiled and took his outstretched hand, feeling the warmth emanating from it. She knew she was going to enjoy working in this lovely place and having the chance to learn more about this man.

★   ★   ★

There was a slight smile on Martin Glover's lips as he sat at his desk and read Juliet's CV for at least the sixth time. There was something about that young lady, with her gleaming dark hair and expressive hazel eyes that had captured his interest. There was a possibility that she might even provide the solution to his problems. It was just a pity that she'd been involved with that business with Sheldon Enterprises and Evan Dean.

He didn't want to be reminded of it, and was sure she didn't either. It had caused a lot of heartache all round. It was time to bury the past and start again. There was a determined expression on his face. Linden Manor Hotel was going places — if he had anything to do with it!

★   ★   ★

Marina returned from her holiday feeling refreshed. She was delighted to learn about Juliet's new job.

'You can stay with me as long as you like, dear, but I suspect you'd like your own place, and it would be more convenient for work.'

They had an enjoyable weekend visiting a National Trust property and a garden centre. Marina promised to help Juliet by making new curtains and cushion covers for her room.

'I've a stack of remnants in the spare room. I'm sure we'll find something to suit you,' she said, studying the sketch Juliet had drawn from memory. 'You're such a talented girl, but I'm sure whatever you do won't be wasted, and you'll be keeping your hand in by sorting out your room. I must admit, I'm as taken aback as you that the staff quarters have been so neglected. It doesn't make for good morale, does it?'

★   ★   ★

Much to Juliet's surprise, Scott volunteered to lend a hand with the decorating. 'I used to help my grandfather during my university vacs. He was one of the old school of painters and decorators,' he informed her.

'You've kept quiet about that!'

'That's because I had my own ideas about what I wanted to do. I've done up my own room and it's not at all bad — even though I do say it myself.'

★ ★ ★

After a week at Linden Manor Hotel, Juliet felt as if she'd been there for ever. She loved being in the country and found the staff very welcoming and friendly. The work was completely different from what she'd been used to, but she certainly couldn't complain that it was boring. Whenever she had any free time, she spent it decorating her room.

She had decided to stick to dove grey and pink, which seemed to be the colour scheme throughout the hotel. Marina had found some material that was exactly right and was busily sewing. Juliet, who was skilled at upholstery, had found some material that would do wonders for the small chair she'd left at her flat in Hertfordshire.

She pushed back her hair and looked up with a smile as Karen came into the room.

'This is looking really great, Juliet. Mind you, it's a pity about the grotty furniture.'

'I can't have everything, and you've got to admit, this is a great improvement.'

'Certainly is. What's through there?'

'I think it must have been a small dressing-room years back. I'm hoping Martin will let me put in a few fittings, and then I can use it as a walk-in wardrobe and get rid of this monstrosity.' She pointed to the enormous Victorian wardrobe.

Karen was waiting for Iain to finish his shift, and then the two of them were going out for a meal. She perched on the bed as her friend worked, and they reminisced about old times.

They were laughing heartily over one

particular incident when Iain arrived and they had to repeat the story all over again for his benefit.

'We'd just finished carrying out the refurbishment to the specifications of the lady of the house, when her husband returned. He'd been working abroad. He said he couldn't possibly live with the colour scheme so we had to do it all over again.'

Karen couldn't tell the story for laughing, so Juliet finished it off. 'No sooner was it all finished than the couple announced they were moving away and putting the property on the market. Believe it or not, it was purchased by friends who had seen the décor as it was the first time round. So, when they moved in, they requested that we changed it all back again!'

The three of them were laughing so much that they didn't hear Martin approach until he said, 'Is this a private party or can anyone join in?'

Karen sprang to her feet. 'Just talking about the good old times at Cramphorn's, Martin. We had some fun ... Right, Iain and I will be off now. We're going out for a meal.'

After they'd gone, Martin continued to stand in the doorway. 'This room is beginning to take shape. Can I give you a hand?'

'You?' Juliet could not hide her surprise.

'Yes, me! I don't mind getting my hands dirty, particularly in a good cause.'

'Then thanks — although,' she surveyed his neat attire, 'you'd better find something older to put on.'

He saluted. 'Right you are, Ma'am, I'll be back in five.'

He returned a few minutes later wearing elderly jeans and a dark T-shirt, and pulled on an overall he'd borrowed from one of the kitchen staff.

'Reporting for duty — what needs doing?'

'This wall needs a second coat.'

They worked in companionable silence for a while, and then he asked, 'So, what do you like doing in your free time, apart from decorating?'

'Oh, you know, the usual sort of things — shopping; dancing, going out for meals, trips to the theatre or cinema and visiting exhibitions. Although I suppose that's a bit limited round here.'

'Mmm, but they do have various functions in the village. They have occasional films and talks in the village hall and visiting theatre groups. If you're interested, I'll get you a programme.'

She stood back to examine her handiwork. 'Thanks, I'd like that. I enjoy walking too, although I haven't done much of that recently.'

He set down his paintbrush. 'So do I, but it's almost impossible to go out with the Ramblers' group, because of working shifts here. Most of their walks take place at the weekends … Perhaps you'd care to join me, sometime, Juliet? I know most of the local walks.'

She smiled at him. 'I'd like that, Martin,' she told him, her heartbeat quickening. 'It's not much fun going on one's own.'

'Not unless you're dog-walking,' he said. 'Although then, I suppose you wouldn't strictly be on your own.'

She laughed. 'No, but you'd have a bit of a one-sided conversation.'

'They used to have dogs here. There's a pets' cemetery in the copse near the staff garden,' he informed her.

'There must be quite a history attached to this place. Marina, Scott's aunt, re-members coming here for garden parties when she was a girl — before it was turned into a hotel.'

He nodded, and for a moment, it seemed as if he was lost in thought; a faraway expression on his face. 'Yes, this place must have been quite something back then. I wonder what the Lord of the Manor would have to say about it now, if he were alive.'

'Oh, I'm sure he'd approve. After all, the upkeep of all those rooms must have been an enormous financial strain.'

He grinned. 'I can tell you've got a sensible head on your shoulders.' He put his hands on his hips. 'This is looking good, Juliet. Surprising what a lick of paint will do.'

She felt a glow of pleasure at his approval. 'It certainly is. Now, I need to think about the carpet.'

Martin wiped his hands on a piece of rag. 'Ah, now I've had a thought about that myself. Come with me.'

Intrigued, she followed him out of the room and down to the ground floor where he unlocked one of the bedroom doors.

She hadn't been in that particular room before. It was smaller than the others she'd seen but beautifully decorated. The carpet was a pink and grey mixture which toned beautifully with the soft furnishings.

He watched for her reaction. 'So, what do you think of the carpet in this room?'

Her feet were sinking into the soft pile. 'It's lovely quality, but I couldn't afford anything like this on the budget you've allocated me.'

He smiled. 'You wouldn't have to. We over estimated; the leftover is stored in the basement, if it's of any use to you? I'm sure our general handyman, Bob, would fit it for you.'

Her face lit up. 'Wow! That would be brilliant! And that would mean I could spend the extra money on some new flooring for the bathroom.'

He touched her arm and she caught her breath at the contact. 'It'll be a palace by the time you've finished.'

They returned to her room to find Scott sitting on the window-seat looking at his watch. He raised his eyebrows when he saw Martin.

'I wondered where you'd got to, Juliet.'

'Martin's been showing me some carpet I can have. He's been lending a hand with the decorating too.'

'Right — I didn't realise painting was your thing, Martin.'

'Ah, well I'm full of surprises,' Martin said lightly.

Scott didn't look too pleased. 'Looks as if I'm redundant.'

'Hardly,' Juliet told him. 'I've left the bathroom 'specially for you. The tin of emulsion is in the bath — rose pink.'

'I'm going to have to push off now,'

Martin told them. 'Duty calls.'

After he'd gone there was a short silence and then Scott remarked, 'You *are* the flavour of the month, aren't you? I don't recall him helping any of the rest of us redecorate our rooms.'

Juliet looked at him appalled, cheeks burning. 'I don't know what you're implying, Scott, but I am aware that this particular room was one of the worst. I chose it because it had potential.'

'Hmm — well, it doesn't do to curry favour with the boss. The other staff won't like it.'

Juliet was speechless and Scott swept up a packet of new brushes and headed off to the bathroom. Just then, Juliet spotted Martin's watch on top of the chest of drawers. Scooping it up, she rushed out of the room, glad of the opportunity to escape for a few moments.

Martin was just coming out of his room on the second floor, looking immaculate once more. 'Oh, thank goodness! I thought I must have left my watch upstairs.'

As he took it from her, his fingers brushed hers, sending a little shiver trembling along her spine. 'Thanks, I wouldn't want to lose it. It belonged to my grandfather, so it's of sentimental value.'

She realised it was the first time he'd mentioned his family.

'And thanks for your help this afternoon,' she said rather unsteadily.

He secured his watch and then looked up, a slight frown on his face.

'You're welcome, but I wouldn't want to tread on Scott's toes.'

Juliet stared at him. 'How d'you mean?'

'He's obviously a good friend of yours and ...' He trailed off as his mobile rang and, after a short conversation, turned to her. 'Sorry, Juliet, there's a crisis in the kitchen — must go.'

Returning upstairs, Juliet went to work on the small dressing-room. She was disturbed by Scott's attitude; obviously Martin had noticed it too. So far as she was concerned, she'd given Scott no encouragement, and they'd only ever had a platonic relationship. She valued his friendship, but if he was going to become possessive she would have to make the situation clear and tell him she wasn't interested.

As she painted, she remembered the night of the party. Scott's parents had persuaded him that it would have been foolish to drive Juliet all the way home, when they could give her a lift. They had tactfully pointed out that he'd probably had a little too much to drink.

On their way to the car park, David and Iris Norris had paused to say goodbye to some friends, and Scott had taken Juliet by the wrist and pulled her behind a large shrub where he had kissed her rather clumsily.

'I've really enjoyed this evening, Juliet,' he'd told her. 'Would you come out on a proper date with me — just the two of us? Dinner perhaps?'

She had found herself agreeing, thinking it was the drink making him behave like that. Now, she realised that he had been serious.

Presently, he came into the room and

stood for a moment watching her paint. 'I'm sorry, Juliet. I shouldn't have said what I did.'

'No, you shouldn't,' she told him sternly, paintbrush poised. 'Particularly as it isn't true.'

He nodded. 'It was just seeing you with Martin ... I realise, of course, there's nothing in it. After all, he's going out with Amanda. So, when can we go on that date?'

Juliet swallowed and decided she was going to have to let him down gently. 'Scott, at the moment, I've got to be single-minded — concentrate on work and getting this room habitable. And next Sunday I've got to pack up my flat in Herts. My landlady's had a couple of enquiries about it.'

He looked disappointed, but then said, 'I bet you could use another pair of hands. If I can juggle the rota, I'll come and help — perhaps we could go for a meal afterwards?'

'OK — that would be nice. Thanks.' She rubbed her neck which was feeling a bit stiff. 'And now I'm going to call it a day. Your aunt will be wondering where I've got to.'

He caught her hands in his. 'You've no idea how delighted I am that you've come to work here, Juliet. I've really missed you.'

She gave him a little smile. 'I've missed you too, Scott, and Karen, of course.'

As she packed away, she wondered how she was going to handle the situation without hurting Scott. She had always looked on him as a good friend — nothing more.

3

Juliet whistled as she replenished the bird feeders outside the dining-room window. It was one of the many jobs allocated to her and she didn't mind a bit. She nearly dropped the bag of bird seed when someone joined in with the tune. Spinning round she saw Martin perched on a garden seat.

'Sorry, couldn't resist. Pleased to know you're happy in your work. Lovely morning, isn't it?'

'Certainly is,' she agreed, and carried on with her task.

'Come and sit down for a few minutes.' He patted the seat beside him.

She obeyed, thinking he must want to tell her something.

'I love this spot and it attracts such a wide variety of birds. The other day I saw a green woodpecker.'

'Really! Have you ever thought of

making a feature of the wildlife round here for the hotel brochure?'

His eyes lit up with interest. 'Now that *is* a good idea. We could certainly incorporate it in our feature on the internet. If you have any more bright ideas, let me know!

'Before I forget, Bob's going to fit the carpet in your room tomorrow and he'll put up those fitments for you so you can use the little dressing-room as a wardrobe. You should be able to move in soon.'

'I'm looking forward to it, and to exploring the countryside. You've whetted my appetite.'

To her disappointment, Martin didn't repeat his offer of accompanying her on a walk. He suddenly seemed preoccupied.

'Right — I've had my breather. It's manic this week. I'm sure you're aware we've got that big wedding on Saturday?'

'Yes, I'll be here, although I'm not sure what I'll be doing yet.'

'Oh, there'll be plenty of work for you. It's an important event for us, so it's all hands on deck. It's the first time we've actually held the ceremony here, so everything has to be just so. A lot's riding on us getting this right. The bride's a model and her father's a local councillor and financier. Her mother's family used to live in the village years back, which is partly why they've chosen us as their venue. They've booked all the rooms for their guests who are staying over, and would have taken more if they'd been available.'

'And there's no possibility of putting any more rooms into use in the future?' she asked carefully.

Martin sighed. 'I'm working on it, but the owners aren't prepared to invest in this place — unless we can prove Linden Manor Hotel is really going to pay its way.'

Juliet frowned. 'But I thought it was doing just that.'

Martin studied his nails. 'To be absolutely honest, it's just about breaking even. There are a couple of other hotels more centrally placed and purpose-built, not too far away.'

'Yes, but as I understand it, they

haven't got the grounds like we have here, or some of the other facilities.'

Martin lowered his voice. 'Juliet, you seem the sort of person I can confide in. I'm sure I can trust you not to say anything about this conversation.'

She nodded. 'Absolutely.'

He hesitated and then said quietly, 'It's my belief that there are those who would love to see us fail. They'd be in their element if they could persuade the owners to sell up. Anyway, I've said quite enough.'

He got to his feet; gave her a little smile, and went through the open French windows into the hotel, leaving her staring after him. She got the impression that he cared a lot about Linden Manor Hotel. She couldn't believe that anyone on the staff would want it to fail. What would be their motive?

★   ★   ★

On Saturday morning, Juliet arrived at the hotel early to find herself called upon to do a variety of different tasks. She had just delivered a basket of fruit and a dozen red roses to the honeymoon suite, when she heard loud shrieks coming from the direction of one of the guest bedrooms which had been allocated to the bridal party to use as a changing room.

Suddenly two small girls hurtled from the room and rushed along the corridor in Juliet's direction. She spread out her arms and they cannoned into her, briefly winding her. A fraught-looking, grey-haired lady appeared in the doorway — presumably their grandmother.

'Rosie! Ruby! Come back here immediately. You really are the naughtiest children.'

The small girls howled and clung to Juliet's overall. 'We didn't do it on purpose. It just happened,' said one of them, tearfully.

Juliet moved forward, with them still holding onto her. It was pandemonium in the room. The matron of honour, obviously the girls' mother, was wringing her hands and the bride was in floods of tears. Another young girl stood nearby, looking as if she wished herself anywhere but in that room.

'They were playing with Lucinda's veil and somehow it got torn,' the older woman explained.

Lucinda sniffed sadly. 'Only it isn't mine, is it? It's a family heirloom belonging to my future mother-in-law. Something borrowed for me to wear and return — preferably in one piece. Flora, I asked you to keep an eye on the girls.'

'They were squabbling over it and it turned into a tug of war,' the young girl said sulkily.

The children's mother clasped them to her and told her sister it was an accident; just one of those things and, of course, they hadn't meant to do it.

Juliet examined the delicate lace veil thoughtfully. It had a large rip in it. She had a sudden brainwave. 'I think I might be able to save the day.' She looked at Flora, who was obviously another bridesmaid. 'Can you take these two into the garden for a run around? I'll rustle up some lemonade and biscuits. The staff will show you where to go.'

The young girl nodded, relieved to escape from the room, and ushered the little girls in front of her.

'Now, I'm going to order coffee and croissants for you all and phone a good friend of mine who's a wizard with a needle and thread,' said Julie, praying that Marina would be in.

She was in — and not only that, but she happened to have a friend over for coffee, who kindly volunteered to drive Marina to the hotel.

By the time Marina arrived, things had calmed down, but it was going to be a race against time to get the veil mended in order for Lucinda to wear it. Marina's nimble fingers flew, and by the time everyone was dressed, the veil was ready. The stitches were so tiny and neat that they were practically invisible.

'I can never thank you enough,' Lucinda said joyfully, and hugged Marina.

Now that the bride had cheered up, she looked stunning and the small girls in their bridesmaids' dresses had been transformed into little pink cherubs. Even Flora was looking happier.

The wedding was a lovely, happy occasion. Marina stayed on so that she could catch a glimpse of the ceremony along with the rest of the staff.

'Of course, nice as this is, I prefer a more traditional church service,' she whispered in an aside to Juliet.

Juliet nodded. 'Yes, so do I, but each to his own.'

Just then, Martin joined them.

'I understand you did a magnificent repair job on the bride's veil, Miss Norris — quite saved the day.'

Marina coloured. 'Oh, I wouldn't say that exactly. We all have our skills and needlework's mine.'

'Yes, I've been admiring the curtains and soft furnishings in Juliet's room. I don't suppose ... Are you completely retired, or would you consider taking on some work here from time to time? We could certainly use your skills.'

Marina was taken aback. 'Well, I er — I don't know. I do enjoy sewing and a little extra cash would come in handy for holidays and such.' She smiled at Martin. 'Why not? Just so long as it's not too demanding.'

Scott came across to join them just then. 'I understand you're quite the star round here, Aunt Marina. That was quick thinking on your part, Juliet. Are you all set for tomorrow, by the way?'

Juliet nodded and Marina said quickly, 'Now, I know you two have got a busy day ahead of you tomorrow, and you're not going to have much time to eat, so I'm going to cook you a roast dinner for when you get back.'

'Oh, but …' began Scott, looking decidedly put out.

'No buts — it's the least I can do and it's ages since you came to me for a meal.'

To Juliet's relief, Scott didn't argue. For a moment, she'd thought he might say he'd already planned to take her out for dinner. She'd realised it hadn't been a good idea to accept his invitation, because she didn't want to give him the wrong impression about their relationship.

'If you'll excuse me,' Martin said. 'I must just check that everything's ready in the restaurant.'

'Does that young man never stop to draw breath?' asked Marina, when he was out of earshot. 'He seems to have the knack of being everywhere at once.'

'Tell me about it,' said Scott. 'The problem is, he expects everyone else to work at the same pace.'

Soon afterwards, Marina's friend arrived to drive her home and Juliet went off to the kitchen to see what needed doing next.

★　★　★

That evening Martin sat in his office doodling on a piece of paper. The day had gone far better than he could have expected. There had been praise all round. Hearing how Marina Norris had come to the rescue had given him an idea. Of course, he would need to think it through, but it might just provide a solution to some of his problems. If only he had the resources, he would finance the project he had in mind himself.

After a few moments he made a decision — one that he ought to have made long ago. There was one person who might be prepared to give him the required backing he needed. He picked up the phone and dialled a number.

'Aunt Jane, it's Martin — have you got time to talk?'

'Martin! How lovely to hear from you. I've always got time for you. Fire away.'

The elderly lady at the other end of the phone listened without interrupting and then, when he'd finished said, 'Yes, you're absolutely right; it's high time I paid a visit to see what's going on for myself. I've left things in Carl's hands for far too long, trusting that he'd make the right decisions. If what you're telling me is correct, then it's time I made a stand. Edwin's allowed Carl to have too much leeway, and I've taken a back seat and left the pair of them to get on with it. I realise now they've not been overly supportive of you.'

'I know that it was your choice to stay in the background, Aunt Jane. After all, it must have been painful for you to hear about all the changes that were going on here,' Martin said gently.

'Yes, it was, but now it's time I came to take a look. The problem is getting to Kent. It seems such a long way from Norfolk, and then there's Toffee. Can I bring him with me? He'll be as good as gold, I promise.'

'Of course you can.' Martin smiled as he thought of Aunt Jane's King Charles spaniel. 'And don't worry about travel arrangements. I'll come and fetch you. Would next Thursday be all right?'

'Yes, dear, if you're sure, but I think it might be best if we didn't mention it to either Carl or Edwin for the time being. Let me see things for myself first.'

'If that's what you want.'

'Yes, Martin, I do. After all, I suspect they don't share everything with me. You know, there is one thing puzzling me about all this.'

Martin shifted his position on the chair.

'What's that, Aunt Jane?'

'What exactly will you gain out of it? I mean you're not likely to have any financial reward like Carl and so ...'

Martin was hurt. 'Aunt Jane, I thought you knew me better than that! Work satisfaction is all I'd ever hope to gain; together with the knowledge that Linden Manor isn't going to be sold to the first buyer with a deep pocket who sees it as a commercial enterprise. I'd hate it to be swallowed up as part of a chain of hotels and to lose its identity.'

There was a pause at the other end of the line. 'Forgive me, Martin. It's just that there must be some reason why you're so attached to the place.'

'I've grown to love it,' he said simply. 'I used to stay around here with my grandparents as a boy, if you remember. My parents were always so busy working that they were only too pleased to let me come here during the holidays.'

'You were fond of your grandparents, weren't you?'

'Yes, I certainly was. They taught me to

appreciate the countryside. This is such a glorious spot.'

'And this girl — the one whose praises you keep singing — do you really think she'll be up to the same standard as Sheldon's?'

He smiled as he thought of Juliet. 'Absolutely! In my opinion we ought never to have engaged them to do the work in the first place. Although, I wasn't here at the time.'

'I can understand why you feel like that, Martin, but do make sure you don't allow your personal feelings to get in the way, won't you?'

'Yes, Aunt Jane. I think I can be relied upon not to do that.'

Shortly afterwards, he put down the phone and stared out of the window. It would be good to see Aunt Jane again and to have her input. Sometimes it felt very lonely in his position. There was no-one he could really confide in here except for Juliet. She had already proved to have a sympathetic ear. He sighed. The problem was, she was involved with Scott Norris

— and he and Scott did not always see eye to eye.

★ ★ ★

Scott had managed to borrow a van from one of his work colleagues, which was a better arrangement than making several trips to Hertfordshire. Juliet left him to put her few small pieces of furniture into the van, together with her books, whilst she concentrated on packing all her clothes into a couple of cases. Her former landlady, Janet, had made them coffee when they'd arrived and had agreed to Juliet storing some boxes in her garage for the time being.

Juliet was amazed at how much stuff she had managed to accumulate during the time she'd been living in the flat. Now that the large wardrobe had been removed from her room at Linden Manor, she could fit in her bookcase together with a small chest of drawers and a nest of tables.

Presently, Scott came to find her. 'I don't know about you, but I'm starving.

It'll be hours before we get our dinner. How d'you fancy brunch at that place round the corner?'

Juliet looked at the chaos surrounding her. 'We-ell, there's still quite a lot to do here ... Oh OK — if you can lend me a hand for the next half hour, we can pack most of this stuff into boxes, and then I'll have broken the back of it. It'll probably still mean another trip next week to get it all sorted.'

Picking up an armful of books, she turned to put them in a box and collided with him.

'Steady!' He caught her in a tight embrace and planted a kiss on her surprised mouth. She extracted herself with difficulty.

'That was not part of the arrangement,' she said breathlessly.

'You must realise how I feel about you, Juliet.'

'I'm sorry, Scott. I value your friendship but I don't have any romantic feelings for you,' she said gently. Seeing his expression, she caught his hands between hers. 'You're a lovely guy, but don't let's ruin our relationship. I'd like us to remain good friends and there must be plenty of girls around who'd love to go out with you.'

Scott didn't reply. Sighing, Juliet carried on with her task. She had never thought of Scott as anything but a friend but then, most of the time he'd been at Cramphorn's, she'd been going out with Evan.

Presently, as they sat over brunch in the pleasant café on the high street, Scott said, 'This wasn't what I had in mind when I asked you out for a meal. Perhaps we can go somewhere a bit more elegant when we both have a free evening — just as friends.'

'Oh, but I'm sure this is just as nice,' Juliet told him hastily, glancing around her at the bright posters adorning the brick-red walls. 'We had some good times in this place when we were working at Cramphorn's, didn't we?'

Scott grinned. 'We certainly did. They were a good crowd — most of them anyway. So, do you think you're going to enjoy working at Linden Manor?'

Juliet paused, fork poised. 'I hope so, after all the work we've put in on my room. You're happy there, aren't you?'

'Yes, of course. What do you make of Martin?'

Juliet stared at him. 'Scott, we've been through all that.'

Scott concentrated on his meal for a moment or two before saying, 'I realise that … What I actually meant was, don't you think he's a bit of a man of mystery?'

Juliet frowned. 'In what way?'

'He's a workaholic; rarely leaves the hotel. No-one seems to know much about him — whether he's got a family. Apart from Amanda, he doesn't seem to have any visitors.'

'I think you're reading too much into it. My family live miles away in Wiltshire, so I don't see them that often — much as I'd like to. Perhaps Martin's live a way off too. It's the way of the world. People have to go where the work takes them.'

Scott dipped his toast in his egg. 'I

suppose so. He just seems a bit reluctant to talk about himself, that's all.'

Juliet thought about Martin for a moment. She'd enjoyed the few conversations she'd had with him, and found herself wishing she could spend more quality time with him. But, of course, there was Amanda.

'Now that I've spent some time getting to know how the hotel works, I'll be based in reception for part of each day,' Juliet informed Scott.

'Won't you find that a bit of a come down after the sort of work you've been used to at Cramphorn's?'

'Not at all. Work is work, after all. I'm not saying I've given up the idea of going freelance with my interior design, but in the meantime I'm quite happy to gain some experience doing something less demanding. Who knows, perhaps I'll be able to do up some of the other rooms. There seem to be enough of them. Anyway, I like the atmosphere at Linden Manor. It's a nice place to work — friendly and welcoming.'

'Hmm.' Scott cut into a tomato and it squirted over his shirt.

Laughing, Juliet passed him a napkin. 'You're worse than my sister's twins! So what did that *hmm* mean?'

'Only what I've told you before — that the owners never put in an appearance. Don't you think that's odd?'

'Oh, there's probably a perfectly reasonable explanation. I expect they're kept fully up to speed with all that's going on.' A thought suddenly struck her. 'Did you meet the owners when you were interviewed?'

Scott shook his head. 'Nope, although a gentleman was there that I've never seen since. Said he represented the owners. Can't recall his name. Expect I could find out. It's probably on my letter of acceptance, if I can find that.'

'It's obvious your filing hasn't improved any since you were at Cramphorn's! So who else was at your interview?' she asked curiously.

'Martin, and Amanda of course.'

Startled, Juliet splashed her tea in

her saucer. 'Amanda! Why ever was she there?'

'Because she was the assistant manager at the time, that's why. Surely you knew that?'

'No — no, it's news to me.' All sorts of thoughts were shooting through Juliet's mind. 'So why did she leave?'

'She was offered the post of Events Manager. She covers the other two hotels in the area. It actually works very well. The Grange is the nearest to Linden Manor. We share some of the evening entertainment, together with events like that Homes and Gardens Fayre you attended here. It's a much more viable and cost-effective way of doing things.'

Suddenly everything seemed to click into place. 'So where is this other hotel, Scott?'

'Oh, a few miles further on — nearly into Sussex. Linden Manor is sandwiched in between the two of them.'

'So, these other two hotels — are they independently owned like Linden Manor, or …?'

'You're not going to like this, Juliet.' Scott paused before replying. 'They're owned by Sheldon Enterprises.'

'What? You're kidding me!' she gasped. 'I'd no idea Sheldon's owned any hotels.'

'I'm afraid they do — since around two years ago. They've always got their eye to the main chance, and when the millionaire who owned the hotels died suddenly, his widow decided to off load them. She felt it was an asset she could do without. Anyway, Sheldon's snapped them up — probably well below the market value.'

Juliet put her hands to her head. 'And I thought I'd left them behind. They seem to be haunting me.'

'It might be some consolation to know that Sheldon Interiors has gone abroad and Elizabeth Sheldon's gone with them.'

'Really! Why haven't you mentioned all this before, Scott?'

He studied the dessert menu. 'Because you didn't ask, and I didn't see the point of saying anything until just now. Anyway, enough of that. Now, I fancy some ice-cream with chocolate sauce on a doughnut. What's it called — a Brown Derby? What about you?'

Suddenly Juliet had lost her appetite. Scott's news had seen to that. Sheldon Enterprises was a huge concern that had managed to drive Cramphorn's out of business, and Linden Manor Hotel was sandwiched in between two of its hotels. No wonder Martin Glover was worried.

4

Juliet wasn't able to do justice to the lovely meal Marina had cooked for them that evening. She was still reeling from what Scott had told her. Afterwards, when Scott had left and Juliet was helping Marina with the washing up, the older woman gave her a searching glance.

'What's wrong, Juliet? You've been very quiet tonight. You and Scott haven't fallen out, have you?'

Juliet shook her head. 'No, it's nothing like that, Marina — it's just something he told me.'

She hung up the tea-cloth to dry and then explained.

Marina pursed her lips. 'Now, why doesn't that surprise me? Sheldon Enterprises seem to have a finger in every pie, don't they? Oh goodness, you don't suppose … Scott is always going on about Linden Manor having mystery owners …'

Juliet shook her head. 'No, although I don't doubt Sheldon's are waiting in the wings.'

'So, let's hope the owners — whoever they are — manage to fend them off. Now, I don't know about you, dear, but I'm ready for my bed.'

Juliet found it difficult to sleep that night. The events of the day kept going through her mind. She intended to speak to Martin Glover at the earliest opportunity.

★ ★ ★

Juliet enjoyed working on reception. It gave her an opportunity to meet the guests. Up until now, she'd just passed the time of day with them in the corridor or when she was dashing off on a task.

Considering Scott had told Juliet that Martin was mainly hotel-based, she found him a difficult man to track down. She was having a well-deserved break in the staffroom on Wednesday lunchtime when he came in.

'Just the person I'm looking for. Layla said I'd probably find you in here. I could do with a chat. I was beginning to think I'd never catch up with you.'

Juliet couldn't help laughing and Martin stared at her in surprise. 'What's so funny — is my hair sticking up or something?' he demanded.

She shook her head. 'No — it's just that I've been trying to catch up with you all this week too.'

'Really?' He looked at his watch. 'Right, it's a lovely day and it's lunch time. I fancy driving out to my favourite watering hole. Would you care to join me? We could call it a working lunch.'

Juliet's heart beat quickened. She tried to keep her voice steady. 'Thanks, I'd like that, although I'd feel rather conspicuous dressed like this. Could you wait whilst I change out of my uniform? I'll only be ten minutes.'

She was as good as her word. She changed into a pair of black trousers teamed with a turquoise-patterned tunic top. When she re-entered the sitting-room, Martin set down the news-paper he'd been reading and smiled at her.

'You look good in that outfit. Right, we'll be off then.'

He took her through the garden entrance and she was relieved not to bump into any of the other staff. They drove along a series of country lanes, bordered by hedgerows dotted with dog-roses. The grass verges were sprinkled with wild mallow and ox-eye daisies.

The pub he took her to was in a secluded spot with the most wonderful scenic views.

'I can thoroughly recommend their toasted sandwiches — they come with side salad and crisps.'

'Lovely, thank you.'

Whilst he was gone, she found a table outside beneath a shady umbrella. A little stream ran at the bottom of the garden. It was idyllic. She leant back and closed her eyes, allowing herself to imagine what it would be like to be going out with Martin on a proper date. She opened them when she heard the sound of ice clinking against the glasses that Martin set on the table.

He stood grinning down at her. 'Sorry to disturb you. I'm obviously overworking my staff.'

She smiled back. 'I wasn't asleep — just day-dreaming. This is such a peaceful spot.' It was a good job he couldn't read her mind!

'Isn't it? I come here when I feel the need to get away and unwind over a nice quiet drink. They don't go in for loud music here. Now, what did you want to talk to me about? You go first.'

Juliet sipped her fruit juice and then said, 'The other day, Scott told me that Sheldon Enterprises owned the other two hotels in the vicinity. Was that what you meant when you said there were those who would like to see Linden Manor fail? I mean, they'd probably be only too pleased to add it to their other trophies.'

Martin looked startled. There was a short silence and then he nodded. 'Yes, that's partly it. You must be psychic!'

She didn't tell him that, initially, she'd thought he'd meant someone on the staff was out to cause trouble.

'So, what we need to do is to ensure the hotel is doing so well that it can't possibly fail. Impress the owner — is that it?'

He raised his eyebrows. 'Goodness! Never mind the owners, *I'm* impressed! You have worked things out, haven't you?'

'So what was it you wanted to talk to me about?'

'Just that, actually. You see, I really need to convince the owners of Linden Manor Hotel that being independent is the way forward. I've seen the sort of work you're capable of — so how would you feel about trying your hand at giving makeovers to a few more rooms?'

'Actually, that was what Karen and I had hoped you'd say,' she told him simply. 'I believe that between us, we could do an equal job to the one that Sheldon's did, at a fraction of the cost.'

'You mean you've already discussed this?' Martin looked incredulous.

She nodded. 'It's by far the simplest solution. Marina could do the soft furnishings. I'll tackle the design and choose the upholstery and we'll all take on the decorating — until you can afford to pay for someone more professional. Bob is brilliant at laying carpets and doing the general handiwork. So, what do you say?'

He grabbed her hand and kissed it. 'I say you're an inspiration, Juliet. Welcome on board as our Interior Design consultant-cum-receptionist.'

The feel of his lips on her hand had made it tingle. She tried not to react. Just then the waitress brought their food and she was glad of the opportunity to compose herself.

'So what do you think?' he asked, watching her intently.

'It's very nice — thanks,' she said, picking up a crisp.

He laughed. 'No, I meant about the job.'

She finished her mouthful. 'Oh, right, I'm sure that'll be very nice too, except …'

He frowned, wondering what she was going to say. 'Yes?' he prompted.

'I would quite like to carry on feeding the birds,' she teased and they laughed.

'You're a funny one,' he said, realising how much he enjoyed her company. 'I'm sure that can be arranged.'

They finished their meal with coffee and portions of cherry pie and ice-cream which, he assured her, was a speciality of the house.

'I realise I'll need to have a staff meeting to put everyone in the picture — but not quite yet. So can we keep shtum about this for the time being? I just needed to sound you out first of all.'

'That's fine,' she said, giving him a radiant smile.

Martin was finding it difficult to think straight. She was such an attractive young woman. Her dark hair was gleaming and her large, long-lashed, hazel eyes shone with enthusiasm. He pulled himself together with an effort.

'Actually, there is something else ...'

'Go on,' she said curiously.

'On Thursday, my Aunt Jane is coming to stay. Actually, she's not really my aunt — she was married to my mother's cousin — but she's been very good to me over the years. Anyway, she's quite elderly now and she'd like to come for a little break. She's keen to see the hotel. So I was wondering if you could sort out a room for her.'

Juliet was surprised, after what Scott had said about Martin never mentioning his family. She dabbed her mouth with her napkin. 'Absolutely. Just let me know her requirements and I'll see what's available. Where does she live?'

'Norfolk, on the coast near Cromer. It's a lovely spot, although it can be a bit bleak during the winter months. Oh, and I should mention that she's got a dog — a little King Charles spaniel.'

Juliet stared at him. 'I thought pets weren't allowed.'

'For this one, we'll make an exception. He's called Toffee, and he's extremely well-behaved. Don't worry; I'll take full responsibility — even volunteer to take him for a walk.'

'Right,' Juliet said with a grin. 'I'll hold you to that.' She laid her spoon and fork neatly on her dish. 'That was delicious, Martin — a real treat. So, have you got a big family?'

'What?' A shadow crossed his face. 'No — no, I'm an only child.'

'My family live in Wiltshire,' she said, trying to draw him out. 'Are your parents …?'

'My mother died when I was at university. My father lives in London,' he said shortly. 'Anything else you'd care to know?'

Colour tinged Juliet's cheeks. 'I'm sorry. I didn't mean to pry.'

He gave a little smile. 'It's OK. I'm sorry too. It's just a bit of a sensitive subject. I was very close to my mother. She'd been ill most of my teenage years and died before I graduated.'

'And did you?' she asked gently.

He nodded. 'Although I didn't get such a good degree as was expected. My father became very remote after my mother's death. If it hadn't been for my grandparents and Aunt Jane, I don't know how I'd have coped. Anyway, enough of me. The problem is you've got a sympathetic ear, Juliet. I find you easy to talk to,' he said gruffly.

She reached out and placed her hand over his. 'That's all right, any time. And you can rest assured, I won't breathe a word to anyone else.'

He sighed. 'I had no intention of saying all that! Anyway, we'd best be making tracks.' He squeezed her hand. 'Thanks for listening. Being at the top in this business can be a lonely sort of place, sometimes.'

What about Amanda, she wondered, as they made their way to the car park. Surely he was able to confide in her?

★ ★ ★

'Whoever is this guest?' Karen asked, as she encountered Juliet, with an armful of flowers, going into the room she'd allocated for Jane Harris. 'She must be important to warrant all this attention.'

'She's an elderly lady who used to stay here years back, so I expect Martin wants to make a good impression,' Juliet told her friend.

'That could be interesting,' Karen said. 'I've often wondered what it was like here years ago. This place must be steeped in history. I'll look forward to meeting her.'

★ ★ ★

Jane Harris turned out to be a petite, frail-looking lady with immaculate silver hair, and an extremely cultured voice. A few glances were exchanged as she entered the reception area with Martin, who held the lead of a small dog.

'Juliet, this is Mrs Harris. Aunt Jane, Juliet will be responsible for looking after your needs during your stay at Linden Manor.'

Jane Harris bestowed a warm smile on Juliet and stretched out her hand. 'I'm pleased to meet you, my dear. Martin's told me quite a lot about you. Now, if you wouldn't mind showing me to my room.'

The elderly lady seemed suitably impressed with her room. 'Goodness, this is a bit different from how I remember it all those years ago! And is that an en suite through there? What an amazing transformation! Martin tells me you're an interior designer — so what made you apply for a job as a receptionist?'

By the time Juliet had told Mrs Harris briefly what had happened, assisted her in hanging up her clothes, and ordered her tea on the internal phone, the time had marched on. Layla was champing at the bit to get off duty.

'Whatever have you been doing, Juliet? I know you've been asked to look after Mrs Harris but surely that's taking things to extremes.'

'I'm sorry, I couldn't get away — you see ...' And Juliet explained.

'What I want to know is whether she's really Martin's aunt and how come she's allowed to bring a dog?'

'She's not a blood relation. She married into his family. Martin told me he'd be making an exception regarding the dog. Apparently, Mrs Harris wouldn't have come otherwise and he thought a few days' break would do her good.'

'Hmm. Well just so long as he remembers we've got other guests to attend to besides her. Right, I'm off now. I'm longing for a swim and I've arranged to meet up with Adam by the pool.'

★ ★ ★

Martin put the phone down with a bang. He was beginning to see another side of Amanda Pearson, although he'd always realised she was a bit self-centred. First she had refused to accept that there was absolutely no way he could manage to take her out whilst his aunt was staying at Linden Manor. Then, when Martin had suggested Amanda came over to meet Aunt Jane at the hotel one evening, she'd chosen to ignore him.

He frowned. And now, when he'd phoned to tell her the musicians booked for that evening's entertainment had failed to show up, she'd calmly informed him that he'd got his wires crossed and they weren't coming until the following week. He scanned the open page of his large desk diary. It was as he thought; Karen was an efficient PA and had definitely booked them in for that evening.

Martin drummed his fingers on the desk. He didn't want to disappoint the guests, but it was too late to engage anyone else. Aunt Jane would think he was incompetent if he couldn't even organise an evening's entertainment!

* * *

Juliet busied herself at the reception desk. She answered several queries from guests, rang for a taxi for a gentleman who needed to get a train, and tracked down a missing suitcase which had been delivered to the wrong room. Scott came to chase up a couple of outstanding bills and stayed to chat for a few minutes.

'What's this about Martin's aunt turning up with a dog?'

Juliet explained all over again and Scott

frowned. 'It'd be interesting to know what would happen if one of us wanted to have a visitor with a dog to stay.'

'Well, at least you might stop speculating about his family now,' Juliet told him sharply.

'But we're still no wiser about his immediate family, are we? Perhaps this Mrs Harris will let something slide.'

'And perhaps she won't,' Juliet said sternly and turned to speak to one of the guests. 'Hello, Mrs James, what can I do for you?'

'I'm afraid my husband's had a bit of a mishap — dropped his towel in the bath. Could he possibly have a clean one?'

By the time she'd finished dealing with the lady's request, Scott had gone. A small boy popped his head over the desk. Juliet smiled at him. 'Hello, Josh, what can I do for you? You haven't dropped your towel in the bath as well, have you?'

He laughed. 'No! It's my mum's birthday today, and my dad and I wondered,' he lowered his voice in a conspiratorial tone, 'that man who plays the music

— could he do *Happy Birthday*?'

'What's this?' Martin asked, suddenly appearing at the desk. 'Taking song requests?'

Josh explained excitedly. Martin rubbed his chin thoughtfully. 'Now that's a tricky one. We might have to ask someone else because I'm afraid the music man and his group are not actually able to be here tonight.'

The little boy looked disappointed. 'Oh. Who will you ask?'

'Whoever it is will play it really well, I promise you.'

'Phew, that's OK then. Thanks Martin.'

Martin bent to the boy's level. 'Does your mum like cake?'

Josh nodded. ''Specially chocolate. Why?'

Martin put a finger to his lips. 'Can you keep a secret?'

Josh nodded again.

'I'm going to see if the chef in the kitchen can make your mum a special cake for this evening. Now, off you go. See you later.'

'Yay!' The small boy grinned from ear to ear and disappeared along the corridor.

'Goodness, that's a bit of a tall order, isn't it? Expecting the kitchen staff to produce a cake at a moment's notice,' Juliet commented.

'No, they've always got cakes in the freezer. I'll pop along and have a chat with them in a minute. That's the least of my worries. The biggest problem is the music. I've only just discovered there's been a bit of a mix-up and the musicians aren't coming tonight after all.'

'Oh, that's a shame. Everyone's been looking forward to the entertainment. Karen said they'd been booked for ages and they're like gold dust. So what's happened? Have they had a better offer?'

Martin thought that, yet again, Juliet had probably hit the nail on the head, but he just shrugged and refrained from making any comment. He'd had his suspicions on more than one occasion recently that the other hotels appeared to take precedence where the entertainment was concerned.

He sighed. 'Think how it's going to look when we tell our guests we've made a mistake with the dates on the posters!'

'Just say the group's double-booked itself, and had to cancel at the last minute.'

Martin nodded and sighed again. 'I don't suppose you happen to have any bright ideas?'

Juliet thought for a moment and then snapped her fingers. 'I've just had a brainwave. Why don't we have a talent show in the ballroom instead?'

'Juliet, you're a genius! Why didn't I think of that? Mind you, would we find enough people to take part?'

'Hang on — we once took part in a show to raise money for charity when we were working at Cramphorn's ... Karen!' Juliet called out to her friend, who was just walking through the reception area. 'Do you happen to have your tap-dancing shoes at the cottage?'

Karen looked startled and then, as Juliet explained, waved her hand in protest. 'Oh, no! That's not in my job description!'

Juliet tried a little persuasion and eventually Karen said, 'Actually, Layla and I have been attending classes at the village hall. If she agrees, then I'm up for it. And, what about you, Juliet?' Karen turned to Martin. 'Juliet's got a lovely singing voice.'

Juliet coloured and Martin said, 'Come on, fair's fair. It was your idea, after all.'

They discussed the programme for a few more minutes and then Aunt Jane appeared at the desk. 'I've worked up quite an appetite. I've just taken Toffee for little walk, and met a dear little boy who told me it was his mother's birthday. I couldn't help overhearing — are you organising some kind of talent contest?'

Martin told her briefly what had happened. Aunt Jane frowned.

'Sounds like they've got a better offer. Well, we'll just have to make the best of it, won't we?'

'It still doesn't solve the problem of the music during dinner, although I suppose we'll have to make do with the usual piped stuff. In a rash moment, I've promised young Josh we'll get someone to play *Happy Birthday* for his mother.'

'Well, that shouldn't present a problem, should it, Martin?'

'How d'you mean, Aunt Jane?'

She slapped him on the back with surprising force for an elderly lady. 'You know perfectly well what I mean, young man!'

Juliet saw Martin redden as he murmured, 'No, I couldn't possibly.' He suddenly brightened up. 'But you, on the other hand, dear Aunt Jane. You could be just the answer to my prayers.'

'We'll come to some arrangement,' she said, and taking his arm firmly in hers, marched away out of earshot.

'What on earth was all that about?' Karen asked, amused.

Juliet shrugged. 'Haven't got a clue, but I've got a strong suspicion we're going to find out! Jane Harris is quite a character, isn't she?'

★   ★   ★

103

Josh came rushing up to the desk after dinner, his blue eyes shining. 'That lady — the one with dog — she played *Happy Birthday* for my mum and it was brilliant. Everyone sang and clapped.'

'Mrs Harris played the piano!' Juliet pretended to be surprised, but Karen had already told her.

'Yep and you should just have seen the cake. It was awesome! It had all this chocolate icing, and one big candle on the top that was like a firework when it was lit.'

'Didn't you save us any?' teased Layla.

Josh rubbed his tummy comically. 'Nope. We've eaten it all — shall I ask Martin if there's another one?'

'I wouldn't push my luck if I were you,' his father said, coming up behind them and winking at Juliet. 'What's he like, eh?' He ruffled his son's hair. 'And now we'd better get you rigged out for this talent contest. It's a good job we bought you that magic set yesterday.'

The talent show was a great success, considering it was an impromptu, last-minute affair. As well as a number of the guests, several of the staff took part. Juliet covered the desk duties whilst Layla and Karen performed their tap-dancing routine to loud applause. After this, one of the catering staff did an Irish jig and Scott was a sensation on the guitar, getting the audience to join in with a medley of popular songs.

'Go and get changed,' Layla told Juliet, presently. 'Everyone's expecting you to do your star turn!'

Juliet hurried into a pair of trousers and a tunic top, and returned to reception to find Martin waiting for her. 'We've got exactly fifteen minutes to come up with a song. I'm supposed to be accompanying you on the piano and we'd better have a practise.'

'What?' she gasped, the colour flooding her cheeks. Catching her by the hand, he drew her into the now deserted dining-room. After a short discussion, they decided to sing a duet from a popular film. They had a quick rehearsal before returning to the ballroom.

Amidst much applause, Martin went across to the baby grand and they put on a performance which practically brought down the house.

Juliet stayed to watch young Josh perform his magic act, and then returned to reception. The evening had gone far better than she could ever have wished for, and she was greatly relieved. She had loved singing with Martin, and wished it could have gone on for ever. She enjoyed being in his company so much, and knew there was some chemistry between them. But then she remembered Amanda!

★　★　★

'It's my belief that our show matched any professional one,' Jane Harris commented as she left the ballroom.

'It was really cool,' Josh said, overhearing this remark.

'Cool!' exclaimed Mrs Harris, placing a hand on his forehead. 'I was boiling hot!'

Puzzled, Josh ran off to catch up with his parents.

5

Juliet was having a hectic morning. Several guests had booked out and others had booked in. She had also been called upon to do a stint in the dining-room during breakfast, because one of the waitresses had hurt her knee. When she returned to reception, she found Mrs Harris patiently waiting for her.

'Ah, Juliet, the very person I need to see. Martin has told me about your lovely room and I was wondering ... I know it's an imposition, dear, but would it be possible for me to take a peep sometime today?'

Juliet gulped and tried to remember what state she'd left it in. She was usually fairly tidy, but she'd been running a bit late that morning.

'Absolutely. Would half past twelve be OK? I'll be off duty then,' she suggested.

'That would be perfect, dear. Will you

come and collect me when you're ready?'

At twelve o'clock, Juliet raced upstairs and hastily tidied away the few things she'd left lying about, including a pile of clean laundry. She checked the bathroom and pushed some shoes out of sight under the bed.

Mrs Harris opened her door so quickly that Juliet suspected she must have been standing behind it.

'I'm really looking forward to this,' the elderly lady announced as they waited for the lift. 'Martin tells me you're a qualified interior designer, and that you used to work for Cramphorn's.'

Juliet looked at her in surprise. 'Yes — you've heard of them?'

'Goodness, yes! I knew Duncan Cramphorn, and his father before him. It was a crying shame what happened.'

The lift arrived and, as they sailed up to the third floor, Jane Harris kept up a constant stream of conversation. Juliet opened the door of her room and waited for the older woman's reaction.

Jane Harris didn't disappoint her. She

spent several minutes looking about her and then proclaimed, 'My dear, this is lovely — equally as nice as my room! To be honest, I prefer it; not so fussy. I'm not really into frills and flounces, although I realise they have their place — in the bridal suite perhaps. That's truly magnificent. Now, what's through there?'

Juliet opened the door of the walk-in wardrobe, and then showed Jane Harris the en suite.

'You and your friends have done a splendid job, my dear. I understand you're hoping to do up several more rooms for the staff?'

'Yes, and I'd also be prepared to have a go at some of the guest rooms. But, of course, I'd need the rest of the team to help me, as they have for this room. I know that Karen would be more than happy to have a go. Actually, she suggested it. Martin doesn't want me to say anything to the others for the time being.'

Jane Harris looked as if she was mulling something over. She crossed to the window. 'I used to love being up here. There's such a lovely view. Oh, the ground floor is nice enough, of course, but this is my favourite.'

'Of course, you used to stay here years ago, didn't you?'

'I certainly did. It was very different back then — no en suites for one thing, just spartan Victorian bathrooms with noisy geysers that frightened the living daylights out of you.'

She paused to examine the newly-covered window seat and curtains.

'I gather another of your friends from Cramphorn's was responsible for the soft furnishings.' Juliet nodded and Jane spotted the chair in the corner that Juliet was still in the process of covering. 'And is this your handiwork?'

'Yes, I'm working on it during my free time. Upholstery was what I set out to do initially.'

'Yes, so Martin was telling me. You'e a talented young woman, Juliet, a real asset to Linden Manor Hotel.'

Juliet coloured slightly, surprised at just how interested Jane Harris was.

The older woman looked pensive. 'Now, I was wondering — do you have time to join me for lunch?'

Juliet thought of the pile of domestic chores she'd planned to do. 'Well, perhaps just this once. I have to be back on duty at two sharp.'

'And you will be. Let's eat outside, shall we? And then Toffee could have some fresh air. Actually, there are one or two things I'd like to run past you.'

Wondering what the older woman wanted to ask her, Juliet ordered sandwiches, salad and coffee at the bar, and then they sat together, soaking up the sunshine on the terrace overlooking the immaculate garden.

Jane Harris folded her napkin. 'That was delicious. Juliet, what you're proposing is admirable, but has it occurred to you that you'd be getting paid a fraction of what Sheldon's received? I mean, why would you be prepared to do all this for such a small remuneration?'

Juliet clasped her hands in front of her, eyes alight with enthusiasm.

'I've only been here a short time, but I've already realised what a lovely, friendly working environment it is. The atmosphere is amazing, and the guests remark on it. If doing this work is going to help persuade the owner that we really care about what happens to this hotel, and prevent it from being swallowed up by Sheldon Enterprises, then that's what I'm prepared to do.'

Jane Harris stirred her coffee thoughtfully. Juliet was a girl in a million and she didn't want to disillusion her. From her conversation with Martin, Jane realised that the younger woman had suffered at the hands of Sheldon's.

'Juliet, I wouldn't want you to raise your hopes too much,' she said at length. 'If the owners of Linden Manor have decided that the best option is to sell up, then I'm afraid they'll do so anyway. Then all your hard work will have been for nothing, and you'd see them lining their pockets with more than they would have done, had you not taken on this project.'

Juliet stared at the elderly lady. 'You

sound as if you know who the owners are.'

Jane nodded. 'I most certainly do. And you're telling me you haven't sussed it out yet? I would have thought you'd have looked it up on that internet search thingummy.'

'I have,' Juliet admitted, 'but all it says is that Linden Manor Hotel is owned by Linden Manor Associates.'

Jane Harris gave a little smile. 'Oh, does it now? Actually, this place is owned jointly by two people — a brother and sister. The brother's an irascible old gentleman who's a bit of a recluse. He leaves the bulk of his decisions to his son, who is rather calculating and obviously hopes to inherit a substantial share one day. You'll have your work cut out, Juliet, to get either of those two to change their minds, once they're made up. So — knowing all this, would you still be prepared to proceed with your plan?'

Juliet swallowed. 'Absolutely — even more so. You see, even if it failed, we'd all know we'd given it our very best shot.

Besides, at the very least, I'd have some more photographs for my book of recommendations, should I want to start up my own interior design business in the future — and that can't be bad, can it?'

Jane Harris had a lump in her throat. This young woman was so sincere, so full of energy and dreams — just as she'd been all those years ago. She patted Juliet's hand. 'Then all I can say is, you go for it, my girl! And I hope you're successful.'

⋆   ⋆   ⋆

Amanda was not in a good mood. She'd received a strange email from Martin, telling her that they'd had a really successful talent show the previous evening. As the Events Manager for all three hotels in the area, she was supposed to be consulted about anything that was to be organised which came under her umbrella, and have the final sanction.

She would have to have a quiet word with Martin and stress this. He was being a bit difficult just recently, refusing to go out with her because some elderly relative of his was staying. And now he was making such a fuss about the date of the entertainment.

Amanda was well aware she'd double-booked the musicians and neglected to tell him, but the manager of The Grange had been very persuasive, and the hotel had been bursting at the seams as a result of it, so it had all been worthwhile. She sighed, knowing she needed to look to her future, and build up her own profile with Sheldon Enterprises.

On the other hand, she most certainly didn't want to fall out with Martin. As a rule they had a good working relationship, and that was proving useful. She'd enjoyed the various occasions she'd been out with him, finding him good company.

A little smile played about Amanda's lips. Actually, there were a number of reasons why she liked to be seen out and about with Martin. No, a firm but gentle scolding — and then a little persuasion to get him to take her out for a drink that evening — should do the trick. Surely his aunt, or whoever she was, could manage without him for a few hours?

When Amanda arrived at Linden Manor Hotel she noticed an elderly woman and a small boy walking a dog. She frowned and, locking her car, crossed the lawn towards them.

'I'm sorry Madam, but I'm afraid the grounds aren't open to the public — only to the guests who are staying here. And I'm afraid dogs are strictly forbidden.'

Jane Harris raised her eyebrows. 'Really? Well, I am staying here and I can assure you that my dog has been made more than welcome.'

A dreadful thought struck Amanda. Supposing the woman was blind and this was her guide dog — although weren't they usually bigger than that? She seemed to remember there was an exception under those circumstances.

Seeing Amanda hesitate, Jane Harris said, 'And, just in case you're wondering, Toffee isn't a guide dog. Fortunately, I can see and hear perfectly well.'

Amanda's cheeks were slightly pink. 'Right. I can only stand by what I've already said. Dogs are not allowed on the premises.'

'Well, this one is, young woman! Might I ask what your position is here? I haven't seen you around before.'

'I'm Amanda Pearson — the Events Manager for all the hotels in the area.'

Jane Harris drew herself up to her full height and stared hard at Amanda. 'Oh, so *you're* responsible for the debacle regarding the cancelled musical entertainment! Everyone felt very let down but — fortunately — Martin and Juliet came up trumps. We had a splendid evening with a homespun talent show.'

'It was brilliant,' Josh informed Amanda. 'We all took part and there were prizes. I did my magic tricks and she played the piano.' He pointed to Mrs Harris.

Feeling at a distinct disadvantage, Amanda decided it would be better to let the matter drop. Things were getting decidedly slack and she'd need to mention the episode to Martin. The woman must have smuggled the dog in without him knowing — that would be it — and now there was nothing to be done.

'Good for you,' she said and began to walk away. 'And Martin Glover or his PA have got their wires crossed,' she called back over her shoulder. 'That musical entertainment is actually scheduled for next week.'

'Bet it won't be as good as ours!' Josh shouted after her.

What a very unpleasant young woman, thought Jane Harris. Surely she wasn't the person Martin had mentioned to her, the one he'd taken out once or twice? If he'd got any sense, he'd ask Juliet the next time round. Unfortunately, Martin had not had much success where women were concerned. Perhaps it was time she gave him a helping hand.

She smiled to herself and young Josh said, 'What's funny, Mrs Harris?'

'If I told you that, young man, you'd be as wise as me and that would never do. Now, I can see your parents waving to you — over there, look, on the terrace.'

'Oh yes, we're going swimming. That pool's awesome. See you later.'

He shot off towards the terrace and Jane went to sit in the shade under a large umbrella. She had a lot to think about and the garden seemed the best place to do it.

*   *   *

Juliet came off duty at nine o'clock that evening, and went into the bar to see if any of her friends were there, so that she could relax over a drink with them. She hadn't dared to hope she'd see Martin, but there he was, sitting in a corner, deep in conversation with Amanda Pearson. Juliet decided not to stop after all. She'd had enough of that particular young woman for one day.

During the afternoon, Amanda had come into reception looking annoyed, and demanded to know the name of the woman with the dog. Juliet had been in the midst of a particularly important call regarding a booking. The booking clerk was having a very late break, and she was standing in for him. She had attempted to mouth this to Amanda who had hunched her shoulders and flicked back her hair.

'I'm sorry, I'm not at liberty to tell you that, Miss Pearson,' Juliet had said pleasantly, when she'd replaced the receiver.

'Don't be ridiculous — I'm a member of staff.'

'But apart from organising the events, you don't actually work here anymore, do you?' Juliet had pointed out politely.

Amanda had stalked off in a huff and, a few moments later, Karen had come up to the desk looking decidedly put out.

'You'll never believe what Amanda Pearson has just had the audacity to say to me!'

'Go on; nothing would surprise me where she's concerned.'

'She's only accused me of entering that musical entertainment under the wrong date in the diary! How could I have done? I've put it on the screen too. Surely, I can't be that daft?'

'Don't worry,' Juliet told her. 'She's had a go at me too. What is she like?'

Unfortunately, Amanda spotted Juliet walking through the bar. 'That's her!' she said to Martin. 'That girl on reception who refused to give me your aunt's name.'

'Juliet? But she was only doing her job, as I've already told you. You, of all people, should know we have a golden rule not to divulge any personal information about our guests.'

'So how was I supposed to know she's your aunt?'

'Amanda, we've been through all that. You've apologised to Aunt Jane and bought her a G and T, and that's an end to the matter, so can we please change the subject?' Martin pleaded wearily.

It had been a long day and Martin had heard several versions of the incident from Amanda, Aunt Jane and young Josh. Amanda had not endeared herself to Aunt Jane, but she had done her best to make amends and the older lady had graciously accepted the apology and the drink. She had not, however, stayed longer in the bar than was absolutely necessary. Having politely made her excuses, she'd returned to her room.

Amanda proceeded to tell Martin about a trip she was planning to Spain with her family. 'My parents have got a villa out there and we all go there most years. Martin, why don't you come? There's plenty of room.'

Martin stared at her for a moment. 'That's an amazing invitation, to stay in a Spanish villa,' he said at length.

Scott, who was walking through the bar at the time, paused by their table. 'What's that? Who's going to be staying in a Spanish villa?'

'I am,' Amanda told him with a wide smile, 'and I've just invited Martin to join me.'

'Aren't you the lucky one,' Scott said with a tinge of envy, and moved away before Martin could reply. Martin knew he'd have to have a word with Scott or it would be all over the hotel.

* * *

Juliet woke early the following morning and decided to go for a swim. When she arrived at the pool, she discovered Martin was already there. 'Come and join me,' he invited, waving to her.

She dived in and swam towards him.

'Great minds think alike. It's wonderful this time in the morning,' he greeted her.

They swam side by side for a few minutes, but she suspected he was a far more powerful swimmer than her, and told him not to hold back. He struck out and after several lengths, came back to her.

'Aunt Jane and I are meeting up for an early breakfast before I go on duty. How about joining us — shall we say in around twenty minutes — unless you want to stay here longer?'

She accepted the invitation with a smile. He climbed out of the pool and reached out his hand. For a brief moment, as he helped her over the side, she found herself surveying his tanned, muscular body gleaming with droplets of water. And then he scooped up his towel from the bench and handed her, her robe.

'I love that costume,' he remarked casually.

She couldn't meet his eyes. Grabbing the robe with a muttered, 'Thank you,' she wrapped it tightly around her. 'I'd better get a move on,' she told him and headed towards the changing room.

* * *

Breakfast was on the terrace. Jane Harris was delighted that Juliet could join them and chattered away like a magpie. 'Martin's got the afternoon off so he's taking me out for lunch, and then we're going for a drive in the country. The weather's supposed to be breaking tomorrow, so we need to make the most of it.'

'That'll be nice,' Juliet said, buttering a croissant.

'I've just checked the rota. It's your afternoon off too, isn't it?' Martin asked. 'So why don't you come with us?'

'Oh, but I'm sure you and Mrs Harris have plenty to talk about,' Juliet protested,

124

her heart beating rapidly. 'Actually, I've promised to take Marina shopping. A neighbour has arranged to bring her to the hotel on her way to visit her daughter.'

Martin turned to Jane Harris. 'You remember I told you Scott Norris's aunt is a friend of Juliet's? She used to work at Cramphorn's with Juliet before she retired.'

'Yes, I've told Scott I know Marina from years back. It would be wonderful to meet up with her again after all this time.' She clapped her hands. 'I've just had a splendid idea. Couldn't you postpone your shopping expedition, Juliet? And then the four of us could go out together.'

Amused, Juliet realised that Mrs Harris was extremely good at arranging things. She knew how much she'd enjoy being in Martin's company that afternoon, and only hoped she wasn't spoiling his plans.

He winked at her. 'What a brilliant idea! But, if you'd prefer to go shopping …'

She coloured. 'Oh, no … I could always stop off at the supermarket when I drive

Marina home. Scott has offered to do her shopping online, but she prefers to choose for herself.'

'She's obviously a lady after my own heart,' Jane commented. 'They tell me it's rather pot luck. I don't fancy ordering a leg of lamb and ending up with a tray of beef burgers!'

'Oh, I don't think it's quite that bad,' Martin told her, a twinkle in his eye, 'although I realise some mistakes are made … So, what do you think, Juliet? Will you join us?'

'I'd love to come,' she said sincerely. 'And I'm sure I can speak for Marina too.'

As Juliet disappeared into the hotel to begin her shift, Martin turned to Jane Harris. 'You do realise, don't you, that things will need to be said, and questions will be asked?'

Jane nodded, understanding exactly what he meant.

★ ★ ★

Marina was dropped off at the hotel at eleven o'clock. She'd arranged to have coffee with Scott whilst she waited for Juliet to finish her shift.

As they sat in the pleasant Orchard Restaurant, Scott said, 'It's a pity I'm on duty today; I could have taken you and Juliet out to lunch.'

'Not to worry,' Marina told him. 'We've received another invitation, from your manager. We're accompanying him and his aunt to lunch, and then having a ride round the countryside.'

Scott's face was a picture. 'First I've heard of it. When was all this arranged?'

'Juliet phoned me this morning. Apparently, I know Martin's aunt from way back, so they thought it would be fun for us to meet up again.'

Scott frowned. 'How come you know her?'

Marina looked a bit vague. 'If it's the same Jane I'm thinking of, then it's from when I lived around here many moons ago.'

Scott stared moodily into his coffee and, after a moment or two, Marina said,

'What's the matter, Scott? You seem a bit distracted.'

He pulled himself together with an effort and gave her a wry smile.

'Oh, it's nothing except … Juliet was glad enough of my company when it came to collecting her stuff from the flat last weekend, but when it comes to going out on a proper date, she's a bit evasive. Martin's already had breakfast with her today, and now lunch … and yet only yesterday evening, Amanda Pearson told me she'd invited Martin on holiday with her to Spain.'

Marina looked thoughtfully at her nephew. 'Is that so? Well, I shouldn't read too much into this afternoon's outing, if I were you. Juliet is such a lovely girl, and she's probably only too pleased to help Martin entertain his aunt — and yours! Anyway, as you've already said, you're on duty so you couldn't have taken us out anyway.'

Oh dear, Marina thought. Scott really was keen on Juliet, but Marina wasn't at all sure it was reciprocated. She picked up her jacket and went off to freshen herself up.

Juliet was ten minutes late getting off duty. She shot off to change and when she came downstairs again, she discovered Marina and Jane Harris in the reception area greeting each other like long-lost friends.

'How wonderful to meet up again after all this time,' Marina was saying. 'Juliet, this is the most amazing coincidence. I knew Jane quite well when I lived in the village, years back. Of course, she was Jane Benfield in those days and not really supposed to be friendly with the likes of us.'

Juliet looked at Marina in surprise. 'I don't understand. Why ever not?'

Jane gave Marina a meaningful look. 'Oh, it was all a long time ago and, nowadays, people would think it was weird but, you see, I lived here in Linden Manor and Marina's father was the assistant gardener.'

The two ladies sank down onto a sofa. 'There was still a class divide in those days,' Marina explained. Before Juliet could ask any more questions, Martin appeared and she had to contain her curiosity.

'Ah, I see you've already been introduced. It's good to see you again, Mrs Norris. Now, we're a bit late setting off so, if you're agreeable, we'll find a nice pub en route.'

The two ladies settled themselves in the back of his white Audi, leaving Juliet to sit in the front. It seemed that Josh and his parents were taking care of Toffee for the afternoon.

'You haven't told us where we're going after lunch, Martin,' Jane said, when he'd been driving for a short while.

'Well if I did that, it wouldn't be a surprise, would it?'

Presently, they stopped to eat at a pleasant restaurant in Goudhurst. It was an attractive village with a duck-pond and a scattering of shops and a steep hill leading up to the church.

'I read somewhere that, on a clear day, it's possible to see sixty-eight towers and spires from the top of the church tower,' Martin informed them.

'Well, you're on your own if you want to climb up there and count them,' Jane Harris told him firmly, 'although I don't doubt it's a spectacular view.'

Martin smiled. 'Another time perhaps, but this afternoon, I've got a treat in store for you. You'll have to wait until we've finished lunch before I tell you what it is.'

Over dessert, curiosity got the better of Juliet. Looking at Jane Harris she ventured, 'I'm puzzled. You said you used to live at Linden Manor, Mrs Harris. I thought you'd only stayed there as a guest.'

Jane set down her spoon and gave Martin a meaningful glance.

'No, my dear, I've been rather economical with the truth. You see, the fact is, it was my home until I was nearly twenty — when I fell in love with the head gardener's son!

'My father was incandescent with rage and cut me off without a brass farthing. Anyway, we were determined to marry and that's exactly what we did — without his blessing.'

'That's amazing,' Juliet said. 'I can't imagine anything like that happening today. Did you ever make it up with your father?'

Mrs Harris shook her head sadly. 'I'm afraid not. He died suddenly — had a massive heart attack. And then we discovered that he was up to his eyes in debt. That's when my oldest brother, Miles, suggested turning the place into a hotel. It was the only way it could remain in the family, and it would have broken my mother's heart to have been forced to sell up.'

'I'd no idea,' Marina said. 'So that was the original Linden Manor Hotel. And then it was sold to the current owners?'

Again Jane Harris shook her head. 'Both my mother, and my brother Miles, sadly died in the same year. My mother had rewritten her will, leaving equal shares to the three of us. Miles had no children, so my other brother, Edwin, and I inherited the entire property.'

'But I don't understand. Why did everyone think it had been sold?' Marina asked.

'Right from the beginning, Edwin didn't have any interest in the place. His son, Carl — who has a silver tongue and is an astute business man — persuaded us that we'd find it a millstone round our necks, and that it would prove more beneficial to sell it. Miles had been an excellent manager and neither of us wanted to take on that responsibility. Besides, I was living in Norfolk, and Edwin and his family had moved to Warwickshire.' Jane sighed. 'So we did actually take Carl's advice and put the hotel on the market. But it turned out the only potential buyer was a builder who wanted turn it into apartments and build a quantity of houses in the grounds. As you can imagine, we weren't having that.'

'Good for you,' Marina said. 'It would have been a crying shame.'

Juliet nodded in agreement, stunned by the revelations.

'So there you have it,' Martin said.

'Now, who's for coffee?'

As they drank their coffee Jane said, 'I might as well finish the story now I've begun it. We had a couple of temporary managers in after Miles died, but they didn't have the commitment, and staff morale was low. Somehow they'd got wind of the fact that the hotel had been on the market, so several of them got other jobs.'

'So you withdrew it from the market and decided to refurbish it,' Juliet said. 'It's beginning to make sense.'

Jane Harris nodded. 'But, of course, we couldn't afford to do too much at a time. We decided to keep quiet about the fact that it hadn't been sold — create a completely new image.'

'Well, you've certainly done that. It's amazing,' Marina said.

Martin looked serious. 'I think Aunt Jane would agree that it would be best if you could keep all this to yourselves for the time being. We're not out of the woods yet.'

'But thanks to you, Martin, we're

getting there.' Jane squeezed his arm affectionately. 'Now, come on — where are you taking us? I'm intrigued.'

There were still a number of unanswered questions buzzing through Juliet's mind as they got back in the car, but she decided enough had been said for one day.

Much to Jane Harris' delight, Martin drove them the short distance to Finchcock's renowned Living Museum of Music. The beautiful Georgian manor housed a collection of restored historical instruments. Jane was in her element. They arrived just in time for one of the informal demonstrations. It was the recitals which made the place so special.

'You couldn't have chosen anything better,' Jane breathed, eyes alight with interest. And Juliet thought again what a lovely, considerate man Martin was.

As they wandered round examining the harpsichords, clavichords and chamber organs on display, Martin pointed to where Jane was being allowed to try out one of the keyboards for herself.

'That's the joy of this place. It's a hands-on museum,' he said quietly.

'It's enchanting. Thank you so much for including us in the invitation,' she breathed, aware of his arm that had linked with hers as if it were the most natural thing in the world.

They finished the afternoon with tea and scones in the delightful Cellar restaurant.

'You couldn't have found anywhere better for me, Martin. It's quite magical,' Jane Harris told him again. 'And being with the three of you has been the icing on the cake. I know I'm going to have to sound out the other people concerned — your nephew being one of them, Marina — but I've got great hopes for the future of Linden Manor. It's my belief that with Martin at the helm, it's going places at long last!'

Martin looked more relaxed than he had done for days. 'That *is* good news. Now we just have to convince Edwin and Carl.'

'You just leave that one to me. We'll

present it as a *fait accompli* when the time comes and, in the meantime, I'd ask you all to keep shtum. Remember Martin, Carl might have a lot to say for himself, but he has no real authority. Trust me,' Jane told him, and winked broadly.

As Juliet drove Marina home that evening, having stopped off en route at one of the smaller supermarkets for a quicker than normal shop, Marina said, 'You know there's one thing puzzling me over all this. Where has all the money suddenly come from? I appreciate there isn't a bottomless purse, but those refurbishments carried out by Sheldon Interiors wouldn't have come cheap.'

Marina had put Juliet's thoughts into words.

'Perhaps they found an old master hidden away in the attic,' Juliet suggested, and they both laughed.

It had been a lovely day, Juliet mused as she got ready for bed that night, and things were definitely looking up. She had loved being in Martin's company. She felt happier than she had done for weeks.

6

The following day, the weather broke and it rained heavily. The guests lounged around the hotel and members of the public poured in for Sunday lunch.

Juliet was roped in to serve the coffees afterwards. Jane Harris beckoned to her. 'I can quite see what Martin means when he tells me you're short-staffed. You have to be versatile in your job, don't you?'

Juliet agreed and poured the coffee. The elderly lady sipped it appreciatively. 'I've been most impressed with what I've seen here these past few days. Apart from you and Martin, no-one knows who I really am, so they're not putting on a show. Anyway, I've decided to keep it that way for the time being — leave Martin to sound people out about the refurbishments. I'm quite prepared to put up a certain amount of money out of my own pocket. I can arrange to pay myself back at a later date, if and when we start to make a healthier profit.'

Juliet could see Scott watching her from the far end of the lounge.

'That's wonderful, Mrs Harris. Now, is there anything else I can fetch you?'

'No, dear, I'm quite comfy here except, I was wondering — I overheard Marina inviting you over to tea and then church, when you come off duty today. She said I'd be welcome too, only I don't have any transport and, apparently, Martin's on duty.'

'Not to worry, I'll give you a lift.' Juliet collected the tray and whisked up some empty cups and saucers on her way out of the room.

'You took your time,' Scott told her. 'You've obviously been entertaining Mrs Harris yet again.'

Juliet smarted at this comment. 'That's unfair, Scott. Everyone has been served. For your information, I've just arranged to take Mrs Harris to tea, and then on to church, with your aunt.'

He looked suitably chastened. 'Right.

Well, just remember we've got other guests.'

Juliet gasped and went off to collect some fresh pots of coffee. Scott seemed to have changed recently. She supposed, if he'd known Jane Harris was one of the hotel's owners, he might have viewed things differently.

It had stopped raining by late afternoon. Jane Harris arranged to leave Toffee behind because of Marina's cat. Martin agreed to keep an eye on him. Marina made them very welcome, although they had to eat their tea rather quickly as the service started at six thirty.

It was peaceful in the Norman church and Juliet was glad for a little quiet, reflective time. Her life had changed so much over the past few weeks, and she hoped she'd made the right decision to stay in Kent. The more she saw of Martin, the more she realised she was falling for him. But she had no intention of stealing him from Amanda Pearson.

And then there was Scott, who had suddenly become quite possessive towards her. Juliet sighed. She seemed to have exchanged one set of problems for another.

Juliet and Jane Harris returned to Linden Manor to find Martin manning reception. He looked up with relief. 'Thank goodness you're back, Juliet. It's manic here.'

'Why, what's wrong? Where's Layla?'

'She's had to take one of the bar staff to A&E. The girl cut her hand on broken glass. Hopefully, it's not too bad. Scott's covering in the bar, but he should have been off duty ages ago. I don't suppose you could do an extra shift?'

'Yes, of course,' she assured him. She hurried upstairs to change back into her uniform and, ten minutes later, took over from a grateful Martin. He gave her hand a gentle squeeze, sending her pulse racing.

'You're a star,' he told her with a smile. 'It's just until Layla gets back.'

Fortunately, Layla wasn't too long. 'Tanya's husband's turned up at the hospital. He'd only just picked up our message because his mobile had been switched off. Right, I'm here now so you can get off. Many thanks.'

'You look as if you're in need of a break, so I'll stay right here until you've had it,' Juliet said firmly. 'Take your time — I'm not in any hurry.'

★　★　★

Juliet was on her way to the lift when Scott caught up with her. Catching her arm, he said, 'Time for a nightcap? I've been wanting a word in your ear and haven't found the opportunity.'

'Can it wait a bit longer, Scott? I'm really tired. It's been manic.'

He grimaced. 'Tell me about it. All the more reason for a bit of relaxation.'

Ignoring her protests, he steered her towards the bar and ordered two glasses of house red. 'Let's go into the lounge. It's rather crowded in here.'

She agreed, uncomfortably aware that Martin was listening from his stance behind the bar.

'OK, I'm all ears,' she said, as they settled in a secluded corner. 'You're looking serious. What do you want to tell me?'

'I couldn't tell you in there — not with Martin doing his barman stint. You two seem to be getting quite friendly. I just wanted you to be aware that he and Amanda ...'

'Oh, is that all?' she interrupted impatiently. 'Scott, I'm fully aware of his friendship with Amanda Pearson.'

Scott sipped his wine. 'Yes, but I doubt if you know this. Amanda's family own a villa in Spain and she's invited Martin to go on holiday with her.'

Juliet was silent, her hands clutching the cool glass. Yes, she'd realised that Martin and Amanda were close, but not so full on as that.

'No, I didn't know *that*,' she said at last, almost in a whisper.

'Thought not, and I'm sorry to be the one to tell you — but I don't want you getting hurt again.' He reached out and placed his hands over hers. 'You see, I care about you, Juliet.'

'Thanks, Scott,' she said lightly, 'but you really don't need to worry about me. I learnt my lesson the hard way last time round — so I'm not likely to make the same mistake twice.'

Scott smiled at her. 'Tell you what, we still haven't had that dinner date so how about it?'

'That would be great,' she told him sincerely; anything to take her mind off things. Yesterday had been such a lovely occasion and, for a short while, she'd allowed herself to dream and have a few romantic notions about herself and Martin. She should have known better. Just then, as if she'd conjured him up from her imagination, Martin came through the lounge, balancing a tray of drinks and Scott called out to him.

'When are you taking Mrs Harris back to Norfolk?'

Martin paused. 'Probably at the end of the week. Why?'

'Oh, I was just thinking about the rota,' Scott said casually. 'So would it be OK if I had some time off on Wednesday evening?

I want to take Juliet out for a meal. I've been promising her long enough.'

Juliet felt her cheeks flush crimson.

'By all means,' Martin told him casually and marched off.

'Good. That's settled then,' Scott said in a satisfied tone. 'How was your outing tonight?'

'What?' Juliet was watching Martin's retreating back, miserably aware that he would now have got totally the wrong impression of her relationship with Scott.

★   ★   ★

'You're looking worn out, Martin. You could obviously do with a break,' Jane told him over breakfast the following morning.

'I wish! No chance of that I'm afraid. You can see for yourself what it's like here.'

'Can't you stay over for a day or two when you take me back to Norfolk?' she asked persuasively.

He shook his head. 'Regretfully, no.

145

Although if we could just get a couple more rooms done up so that we could employ more staff — well, then it might make enough of a difference that perhaps I could take a break. Sometimes, Aunt Jane, I feel as if I'm fighting a losing battle.'

Jane Harris patted his arm. 'Oh, don't say that, dear. Let's give it our very best shot before we admit defeat. You certainly have my vote — just remember that. Why don't you take that lovely girl, Juliet, out for a meal?'

He looked at her in surprise. 'Because *'that lovely girl, Juliet,'* is already going out with Scott Norris. She's known him for a number of years. He's taking her out for dinner on Wednesday.'

Aunt Jane looked disappointed. 'Well, you could always change the duty roster and take her out yourself.'

Martin had to laugh. 'Aunt Jane, I'd no idea you were so devious! No, if I take anyone out, it'll be Amanda Pearson. We're long overdue for a business discussion.'

'Hmm,' Aunt Jane said disapprovingly. 'I have to admit she wouldn't be my choice of a companion for you.'

'It'll be a working lunch,' he informed her with a smile. 'Now, I'm afraid I must get on. I've got a busy morning ahead of me. At least the weather's brightened up.'

'I'm going to get a taxi into the village,' she told him. 'It's high time I took a look around some of the old haunts. Who knows, I might encounter one or two people I know. Don't look so alarmed, Martin, I'll be careful what I say.'

Back in his office, Martin picked up the phone to call Amanda. He needed to talk to her about her invitation to Spain. He would let her down gently — tell her it was impossible for him to get away. He had to admit that for a short while he'd considered accepting — the thought of getting away for a couple of weeks was tempting. But it would have been wrong to lead Amanda on. She was fun to be with — if a little demanding sometimes — but nothing more. She was a lively girl, a bit of a party animal. He, on the other hand, preferred a quieter lifestyle. He sighed as he thought of Juliet. Now there was a girl after his own heart.

'I'm sorry, Amanda, but I can't manage anything other than a working lunch this week, and it will have to be today,' he told her firmly. 'I'm taking my aunt back to Norfolk on Thursday so you can imagine how busy I am.'

'Really, Martin, you're no fun these days. OK then lunch it is. Where?'

'Shall we meet at The Grange?' he suggested. He hadn't been there for a while and could weigh up the opposition.

After he'd put the phone down, he sat staring into space for a few moments, his thoughts turning back to Juliet. He couldn't seem to get her out of his mind. She was, as his Aunt Jane had described her, a lovely girl — talented too.

* * *

Amanda took Martin's refusal to accompany her to Spain better than he'd expected. 'Oh well, it's your loss,' she told him as she ate her panini. 'Now, about this evening's entertainment ...'

After lunch she whisked him off to take a look at the state of the art conference room, and all the latest technology it boasted.

'Brilliant, isn't it?' she beamed at Martin. 'Sheldon Enterprises are going from strength to strength. You know something Martin, if you don't watch out, Linden Manor will be left behind.'

Martin bristled. 'At least Linden Manor's got its own individual character. And whatever Sheldon Hotels might have to offer, they simply haven't got the grounds for weddings and garden shows!'

Amanda caught his arm, realising she'd gone too far. 'You're right there. I was only teasing. You're becoming too serious these days, Martin ... Hi Jamie.'

She broke off to greet a tall, blond-haired young man dressed in expensive -looking sportswear. 'Now, is there anything else we need to discuss, Martin? Jamie and I are putting together a leisure package for our special weekend deal. You should try out the gym here sometime, it's amazing! Thanks for lunch — see you later.'

★　★　★

Before he went to Norfolk, Martin held a meeting with the staff who had volunteered to help with the refurbishment of the extra staff bed-sits.

'As most of you are aware, Juliet has experience as a qualified interior designer. So, as I'm sure you'd agree, it would make good sense to use her expertise.'

There was a general murmur of agreement.

'How's it going to be funded?' asked Iain, in his usual forthright manner.

Martin looked slightly taken aback. 'Oh, you've no need to concern yourself about that. Let's just say there's a small amount of money available for emergencies, and I'm going to put it to good use. You'll all receive some overtime pay too. Now, before you commit yourselves, shall we take a look at the rooms concerned?'

The two rooms he had in mind were

further along the corridor from Juliet's. He flung open the door of the first one.

'Goodness, this is in a bit of a state,' Layla said, surveying the peeling wallpaper and ancient curtains. 'And I can't see any sign of an en suite.'

Martin grimaced. 'No, 'fraid not. There's a bathroom in between the two rooms. That would have to do for the time being. So what do you think? Could you do something to transform this?'

'It would certainly be a challenge,' Juliet told him with a grin. 'My room is quite palatial in comparison with this.' She was already making mental notes. 'Marina could make a start on the soft furnishings. And is there any more of that carpet available?'

Martin grinned at her enthusiasm. 'Possibly. Now, let's take a look at the other room, shall we?'

If anything the room next door was in an even worse state than its neighbour. Everyone stood in silence for a moment or two, looking around them.

'The saving grace is the view from this

window,' Iain said at length.

Juliet frowned in concentration. 'I'll need to come back and make a few comprehensive notes. It would be cheaper to use emulsion rather than wallpaper. OK Martin, I'm prepared to give it my best shot, but setting these rooms to rights will be more expensive than mine was.'

'Fair enough, we've got a bit more money to play with now — although we can't be too extravagant. Now, can you brace yourselves to look at the bathroom?'

When the others went back on duty, Juliet remained behind to discuss a few more details with Martin.

'There is one important thing to consider, Juliet. If you're on reception most of the day, it will be difficult for you to fit all this in.'

She nodded. 'Yes, I realise that. What do you suggest?'

'How would it be if I employed some temporary help for a couple of mornings a week? There's someone in the village, Kirsty Jones, who's always keen to step in. She's got young children, so she can't help out on a more permanent basis.'

Juliet nodded. 'That sounds like a good solution. Tell me, are the rooms you've designated for extra guests as bad as this?'

'Fortunately, no, because they've always been guest rooms. D'you want to take a look at those too?'

'Might as well. Then I'll have a better idea of what needs doing.'

Juliet followed him down to the second floor and along another corridor. He unlocked the door of the first room. When they stepped inside, she caught her breath. It was old-fashioned and in definite need of a makeover, but there was so much potential.

'This is more like it,' she said, eyes shining. 'We could have rose-coloured walls and soft furnishings, white paintwork and a darker pink carpet. Can I see another couple of rooms?'

Further along the passage the rooms were a little smaller, but they were in reasonable condition too. She stood looking at the last one, deep in thought.

'Juliet, whatever's wrong?' Martin

asked at length, touching her arm.

She started, feeling as if she'd just received an electric shock. She pulled herself together with an effort. 'Nothing. Quite the reverse, actually. I've just had an idea I'd like to run past you.'

'Go on.' He looked at her intently but, just as she was about to share her idea with him, his mobile rang. With a muttered exclamation he snatched it up. 'Yes, Karen. OK, I'll be with you in a couple of minutes,' he said rather irritably, and turned back to Juliet. 'Sorry, got to go — mix-up over a guest's bill. Catch up with you later.'

Feeling frustrated, Juliet spent the next hour or so working on her ideas for the makeovers and then went back on duty.

Layla was full of the meeting. 'I think it's a great idea to do up those rooms. I'm all for it, especially if it means getting the extra staff more quickly. Paying us overtime is providing just the right incentive. When do we begin?'

'I just need to run something past Martin first of all. Also, I'm not sure if he'd want us to get started unless he's around to supervise.'

Layla frowned. 'I thought you were in charge of the project. Surely the sooner we begin, the sooner we finish. Although I suppose if Health and Safety got wind of it they'd have a field day.'

Juliet clapped her hand to her mouth. 'Oh, help — I hadn't thought of that. Right, we'll just have to take extra care then, won't we?'

★ ★ ★

That evening, Juliet sat over a solitary meal in the area of the dining-room allocated for the staff. It had been a busy shift on reception and she was looking forward to a nice long soak in the bath and an early night. Suddenly she saw Martin heading towards her bearing a tray with a large bowl of strawberries, a jug of cream and coffee.

Juliet gaped at him as he set it down on the table. 'How did you get those straw berries? Chef told me there weren't any left.'

He grinned. 'Ah well, you have to know how to work the system. I had my main course with Aunt Jane, but didn't have time for dessert so I asked him to put some by for me. Mind if I join you?'

'Of course not — especially if you're going to share those!' She put the magazine she'd been reading to one side.

Martin collected a couple of cereal bowls from the breakfast buffet and doled out the strawberries. 'Come on then — I've waited quite long enough to hear about this idea of yours.'

'Oh, it's quite simple really,' she told him, helping herself to cream.

'Those guest rooms on the second floor are obviously in much better shape than the ones you're thinking of doing up for the extra staff — so why don't you advertise for a couple more live-in staff right now, clean up those guest rooms and put them in there for the time being? That'd give us more time to make the rooms on my floor habitable. If the new staff used the first two, we could work on the furthest one. Except ...'

'Go on,' he prompted, eyes alight with interest.

'Actually, I think we should be more professional regarding the decorating of the guest rooms. I was chatting to our handyman the other day and apparently, his son-in-law's a decorator and not overly busy at present.'

Martin swallowed a mouthful of strawberry. 'Let's get this straight. You suggest we put two staff members in the guest rooms on the second floor and, in the meantime, do up one other guest room in addition to the extra staff bed-sitters?'

'Yes — and the en suite and that dreadful bathroom, of course. That way we get the best of both worlds. Otherwise, it's a vicious circle — no room at the inn for anyone. We can't take on extra guests without extra staff. We're pushed to our limits as it is.'

'Goodness, you've really thought this through, haven't you?' he said in admiration. 'Ready for coffee?'

She nodded. 'Those strawberries were delicious. Shouldn't you be entertaining your aunt?'

'No, she's entertaining the guests by playing the piano so they can dance. Scott's supervising. He's much better at that kind of thing than I am. Everyone's having a whale of a time, old-time dancing!'

When they'd finished their coffee, Martin yawned. 'Sorry! I could do with some fresh air. Feel like coming for a walk? We won't be missed.'

Her heart leapt. 'Love to. Can you give me a few moments to fetch my coat? Oh, but what about Toffee — does he need a walk too?'

'No, just us. Josh and family took Toffee for a long walk before dinner and the poor little chap's worn out. Apparently, he's sound asleep in his basket.'

Martin couldn't imagine Amanda being so concerned about his Aunt Jane's dog.

Juliet hurried back to her room and changed into something more suitable for a walk. She hastily splashed water on her face, and did a running repair to her make-up. A short walk in the grounds with Martin appealed to her far more than the meal she was to have with Scott the following evening.

Every time she thought about it she was filled with apprehension and wished she hadn't accepted his invitation. She scolded herself for being so mean; he was a good friend and she mustn't forget that.

Martin and Juliet had a short walk in the copse. The light was fading and Juliet suddenly caught her foot on a tree root. She stumbled, and a moment later, found herself clasped in Martin's strong arms.

'Steady,' he cautioned, 'I can't do without you.'

She knew he was only referring to work, but his closeness sent her pulse racing. She could feel the warmth of his muscular body pressing against her, and smell his cologne — like a fresh mountain spring. For a long moment she stayed there in the shelter of his arms.

'Thanks,' she said breathlessly. He retained her hand in a warm clasp as they made their way back through the copse.

The leaves formed a canopy overhead and, now and then, a rustling alerted them to wildlife.

'I wouldn't like to be here on my own,' she admitted.

'I used to know these woods like the back of my hand when I stayed with my grandparents.'

'What did they do?' she asked curiously.

'My grandmother was a cook for the Benfields and my grandfather was a carpenter. There was always a lot of work to be done. They lived in a cottage belonging to the estate ... Listen! Can you hear the owl?'

They came out of the copse, and she realised he was still holding her hand. The unexpected intimacy sent a warm glow pulsating through her.

'Do you want to go back now or shall we sit in the staff garden for a little while?'

'That would be lovely,' she told him. It would remind her of the evening of the party when she'd encountered him sitting there.

'We seem to enjoy a lot of the same

things,' he said as they strolled round the garden. The summer scents were intoxicating; night scented stock, roses and lavender.

'I was thinking that too,' she told him, wishing the evening could go on forever. 'Sometimes I wish the world would slow down. Everyone's going at such a great pace, but here it's as if time has stopped still. It would be such a pity to spoil it, Martin.'

'Yes, it would, and I'm going to do everything in my power to prevent it from happening. You're a girl after my own heart, Juliet Croft.' And cupping her chin between his hands, he kissed her gently on the mouth.

For a long moment it was as if her dream had come true and then he said softly, 'That's a thank you for being you. If things were different then — perhaps ...'

'Yes,' she sighed, remembering Amanda.

7

Juliet hummed to herself as she painted the undercoat on one of the walls in the room designated for a new member of staff. She jumped when a pair of hands caught her round the waist.

'Scott! I thought you were on duty.'

'I've got some time off for good behaviour,' he told her with a grin. 'So I wondered if you needed a hand.'

'That would be great, thanks. The sooner we get this room done, the better.'

'You haven't forgotten our dinner date this evening?'

'As if! There is one thing though — where are you taking me? I need to know what to wear. Is it smart casual or more glam?'

He picked up a paintbrush. 'It's a surprise — smart casual will be fine.'

Juliet found herself wishing that the dinner date had been with Martin. The kiss had made her realise the extent of her feelings for him. She knew that it had played chaos with her emotions, and was glad that he was going to be away for a couple of days. She'd done her best to avoid him that morning. Scott cut across her thoughts.

'Pardon me for mentioning it, but shouldn't the ceiling have been painted first?'

'Strictly speaking, yes, but Martin's asked Bob's son-in-law, Jim, to do it — so we've arranged that it'll be OK just to put the undercoat on the walls. Jim's making a start on one of the guest rooms this morning.'

Scott's face was a picture. 'He's doing up one of the guest rooms! So when was all this decided? Martin hasn't mentioned it to me.'

'Really? Well, I'm sure he will before long.' Juliet hoped she hadn't put her foot in it. She'd assumed Martin would have told Scott by now. 'Actually, it was my idea.' She filled him in. 'Karen's doing an ad for the local papers for additional members of staff, even as we speak. Obviously, she'll be putting it online too.'

Scott frowned, 'Right. I'd like to know where all this extra money is coming from all of a sudden.'

'Can't help you there,' she said, wishing she didn't have to be so economical with the truth. 'I do know your aunt has got sufficient material to do out this room. She's got a lot of contacts from working for Cramphorn's for so long, so doing up another guest room or two won't come to anything like as much as it did when the owners used Sheldon Interiors.'

'I should hope not! Speaking of my aunt, she's on the terrace having coffee with Mrs Harris.'

'Yes, I know. I collected her earlier on so that she could do some measuring up — curtains and such-like. Jane Harris is going home tomorrow, so they won't be seeing each other for a while.'

'I see. It would be nice to be kept in the loop,' he said, sounding disgruntled.

Juliet felt uncomfortable. 'Sorry, Scott. I would have told you, but I haven't had the opportunity. D'you fancy a coffee? I'll just nip along to my room and put the kettle on.'

When Juliet returned with two mugs of coffee and a packet of chocolate digestives, she found Scott talking with Bob who'd come to fill in some cracks and take a look at the ceiling.

She handed over both coffees and was about to go and make another for herself when Bob said, 'I've only just realised who that Mrs Harris is. It was seeing her talking with your aunt, Scott.'

'Sorry, Bob — I'm afraid you've lost me. Mrs Harris is Martin Glover's aunt, isn't she?'

Bob helped himself to a chocolate digestive. 'Some sort of cousin, as I understand it, but that wasn't what I meant. She was Jane Benfield and used to live here in Linden Manor.'

Scott looked puzzled. 'How d'you mean — used to live here?'

Bob swallowed his mouthful. 'Well, it was her folks who owned Linden Manor. Then, after her father died, they were responsible for turning the place into a hotel. That's how she knows your aunt from way back when they were children.'

'First I've heard of it,' Scott said, looking thoughtful.

'Family history isn't really your thing, is it?' Juliet cut in, hoping they could change the subject. 'So, what d'you reckon, Bob? How long will it take to put this room to rights?'

'Oh, just a few days. Once we get these cracks filled in and the ceiling done, it'll be plain sailing. It'll be great to see some of these rooms put to good use again.'

Bob was not to be put off so easily. He helped himself to another biscuit and munched it thoughtfully. 'You might not know this, Scott, but your Aunt Marina was sweet on one of those Benfield boys.' He scratched his head. 'Now, which one was it? I was only a youngster at the time, but I distinctly remember my old dad telling me once, when we were looking at some photographs.'

Scott seemed lost for words.

'How's Jim getting on downstairs?'

166

Juliet asked, attempting once more to steer the conversation onto safer ground. Much as she found the conversation interesting, she was sure Marina wouldn't want her love life to be discussed with her nephew.

Eventually, Bob went off to collect some more filler and Scott turned to Juliet. 'I suppose you knew about that, too?'

'Not all of it, no,' Juliet assured him, 'and if I were you, I wouldn't listen to idle gossip. Now, would you like another coffee? I'm going to make one for myself, seeing as Bob's just drunk mine.'

*   *   *

'I've had a very worthwhile morning,' Marina told Juliet as they lunched together in the garden. 'I've got lots of ideas for the soft furnishings and had such an interesting chat with Jane Harris. She's been telling me all about her life in Norfolk. Such a shame her husband died so young. They were so very much in love

... This soup is amazingly good. Do you think Chef would give me the recipe?'

'I'm sure he'd be flattered.' Juliet helped herself to some more crusty bread and reached for the butter. 'It must have been quite a culture shock for Mrs Harris when she left this place.'

'I'm sure it was, but her godmother was very good to them. She lived in Norfolk, which is why they went there. Eventually, they inherited quite a large sum from her estate, so Jane was telling me.'

That answered a few questions. After all, Jane Harris hardly seemed hard-up. 'Bob, our handyman, was saying he remembered Mrs Harris from years ago,' Juliet said casually.

'Yes, I expect he would do.' Marina gave Juliet a quizzical look. 'And, did he happen to mention that I'd had a fling with Miles Benfield?'

'Well, no,' Juliet replied honestly. 'He didn't actually use the word *fling*, and he couldn't remember which of the brothers you'd, er, gone out with ...'

Marina laughed and dabbed her chin

with her napkin. 'Bob would only have been a small boy at the time, but I expect his father would have told him in more recent years. I was only seventeen and Miles was a couple of years older. We met at the church youth club. Young love is a wonderful thing, but it can cause a lot of heartache, as I'm sure you'd agree. It wasn't long before we were separated. My parents told me we were moving to live with my grandfather, whose health was failing. Soon afterwards, Miles went off to college. We kept in touch for a time, but somehow we drifted apart.'

'And neither of you ever married?' Juliet prompted gently.

Marina shook her head. 'Work overtook. I went to work at Cramphorn's, and Miles eventually came back here to manage the estate, and later, the hotel. No-one special came along for either of us. Oh, well; it's no good dwelling on the past and what might have been ... Now, how about some coffee? And I fancy raspberries and ice-cream.'

'Oh, I'm not sure I should — I'm going

out to dinner with Scott tonight.'

'Yes, I know, but a few raspberries won't hurt you. I did ask Scott to join us, but he's had to go back on duty. It'll be a relief all round when you get some additional staff here. At present, everyone seems to be roped in to do just about everything.'

Juliet was feeling rather guilty over several things where Scott was concerned. She rested her elbows on the table and told Marina, 'I think Scott might be feeling a bit left out of things. He didn't realise this was Mrs Harris's childhood home.'

'And was he around when Bob mentioned my little fling with one of her brothers?'

'I'm afraid so.' Juliet beckoned to a passing waiter and gave their order.

'Not to worry. He's offered to drive me home later. I'll explain a couple of things to him. Have a good evening, won't you?'

'We will,' Juliet rejoined lightly, even though she wasn't too sure about the evening ahead. As she tucked in to the raspberries and ice-cream, she said, 'You know, I'm still not clear how Martin's family are connected with Mrs Harris. I mean I'm aware his grandparents worked for the estate, but how does that make his mother Jane Harris's cousin?'

Taking a pen from her bag, Marina drew a rough family tree. 'You see, Martin's grandfather had a brother, Joe — Martin's great uncle. It was his son, John, who married Jane Harris, or Benfield, as she was then. As she mentioned the other day, John was a gardener on the estate. Martin's mother, Sarah, and John were first cousins. Does that make sense?'

'Mmm, I think so. Martin told me Jane Harris had been very good to him when his mother had died. I don't think he sees much of his father nowadays.'

Marina dipped her last spoonful of ice-cream into the raspberry juice. 'Yes, that's a great pity; and now that his grandparents have also passed away, he's very much on his own. Jane is very fond of him, and appreciates what a great job he's doing here at the hotel.'

Juliet nodded. 'His heart's really in it, and he's so keen to make these improvements work.' She glanced at her watch. 'Oh my — I've got exactly fifteen minutes to drink my coffee, change into uniform and relieve Layla on reception.'

★ ★ ★

Scott took Juliet to an upmarket hotel and country club for their evening meal. Her eyes widened when she saw the menu and she realised just how costly it was going to be.

Seeing her hesitate, Scott said, 'I've got a confession to make. I was given a couple of vouchers from one of our suppliers. It happens sometimes. Hope you don't think I'm being a Scrooge, but it's actually for the set menu.'

'Hardly! This is an unexpected treat,' she assured him. 'I just hope I'm dressed for the occasion. This place is rather more opulent than I'd anticipated.'

His eyes swept over her, taking in the

172

coral-pink dress with its shoestring straps and ruched bodice. 'You look fabulous.'

'I wasn't fishing for compliments,' she told him, colouring, and turned her attention back to the menu, studying the set one this time. She chose a mushroom starter, followed by grilled salmon with a red pepper sauce and seasonal vegetables. The food was good, but Juliet decided she wouldn't rate it as high as Linden Manor Hotel.

Scott went out of his way to be a charming and attentive companion that evening. He was quite an extrovert and could be very amusing when he chose. Juliet relaxed and began to enjoy herself.

'Bob was right, you know. Aunt Marina was telling me she used to go out with Miles Benfield — Jane Harris's brother. Whoever would have thought it?'

'Mm, life's full of surprises,' Juliet said and gasped. 'And here's one of them!'

Amanda Pearson had just walked into the restaurant wearing a short, lime-green dress that showed off her long legs and curvaceous figure to advantage.

'What? Where?' Scott followed her gaze. 'I don't believe it — Amanda! What is she wearing? That dress is very, um ...'

'Eye-catching?' Juliet suggested, wickedly.

Scott coloured. 'I was going to say dazzling.'

'Who's that guy with her?' Juliet asked, noticing the tall, blond-haired Adonis that took her arm.

'Oh, that's Jamie Parrish — the chap who works at the leisure centre at The Grange. He's related to the manager. I went on a course with him once. Bit of a know-it-all. Wonder what Amanda's doing out with him?'

'Same as us — enjoying herself, I expect. Perhaps he's got some complimentary vouchers too.'

'Look, there's another guy with them,' Scott said slowly. 'See? He's already seated at that table in the window alcove. That's strange. I've got a strong feeling he's the guy that interviewed me — the one I told you about, whose name I can't remember.'

Juliet looked in the direction of the table Scott had indicated. The third member of the party, dressed in a dark grey suit with a pale blue cravat, was considerably older than Amanda and Jamie, and Juliet didn't recognise him at all. She had a feeling that this was no ordinary dinner party.

'Oh, if only I could remember his name,' Scott said, pressing his hand to his head. 'I'll ask Martin when he gets back from Norfolk. Mind you, he might not be too pleased to learn Amanda's been out with Jamie.'

'Don't tell him then,' Juliet advised. From where she was sitting she had a good view of Amanda's table. There was a lot of talking and laughter, and Jamie seemed very attentive to Amanda, placing an arm about her shoulder as they studied the menu together.

Just then the waiter came along with the dessert trolley. Scott chose sticky toffee pudding whilst Juliet asked for a portion of strawberry pavlova. She had to prevent herself from glancing at the other table, and noticed that Scott was doing the same. He suddenly seemed preoccupied and she wondered what he was thinking about.

'I'd very much like to know what's going on there,' he said abruptly, as he tackled his pudding.

'Oh, we're probably making something out of nothing,' Juliet said. 'Just because that chap has some connection with Linden Manor, there's no reason why he shouldn't be friendly with Amanda and Jamie, is there?'

Scott shrugged. 'No, I suppose you're right … The thing is, Juliet, I don't altogether trust Amanda. She's capricious. Ever since I've been there she's been bombing in and out of Linden Manor as if she owns the place and is checking up on us. I know she was assistant manager before me, but that doesn't give her the right to throw her weight about now.'

'No, I know what you mean. She can be a bit full on,' Juliet agreed, remembering the incident with Jane Harris's dog. 'Layla told me everyone was taken aback when she left to take up the post of Events Manager.'

'Yes. I've heard that. Anyway, I wouldn't be in the job but for her quitting.'

'That's true and you seem to like it well enough.'

Scott considered. 'As a stepping stone, yes. I'm gaining a lot of experience, but at times I find it a bit restricting. I don't intend to stay there forever ... Don't mention that to Aunt Marina or Martin, will you?'

Juliet set down her spoon. 'Of course not — what do you take me for? So, what do you want to do with your life?'

Scott leant back on his chair. 'Oh, something in management. I like Linden Manor well enough, but it's a bit out in the sticks for me. I'm missing the town life. I realised that when we went back to Herts to collect your stuff. And then there's all this uncertainty about whether the hotel's going to remain independent. If it were to be taken over by a group it'd lose its individuality. Who knows? I might go abroad for a spell — fancy coming with me?'

Startled, Juliet was silent for a moment or two. She stared at Scott, trying to decide if he were being serious. 'You're full of surprises, Scott. So, what's brought this on?'

'Tell you over coffee. Can we sneak into the lounge without those three noticing, d'you suppose?'

They found their way into the lounge from the back of the restaurant, and sat in a secluded alcove.

'That was a lovely meal, Scott. Thanks a lot.'

'My pleasure. Mind you, that sticky toffee pudding wasn't a patch on our chef's.' Scott suddenly snapped his fingers. 'It's Carl! It's just come to me.'

'Whatever are you talking about, Scott? Who's Carl?'

'That chap with Amanda and Jamie is called Carl someone-or-other. I've looked at him several times, and I'm more convinced than ever that he was the man who interviewed me.'

Juliet swallowed. It was one of those moments when she didn't know whether to speak or remain silent. She suddenly remembered that Edwin Benfield's son was called Carl.

The name Carl Benfield had obviously meant nothing to Scott when he'd been interviewed and, anyway, Carl wasn't one of the owners. If it *was* Carl Benfield sitting at the table with Amanda and Jamie, then Jane Harris hadn't been aware he was in the area.

Juliet decided it would be more prudent to keep shtum until she'd had the opportunity to speak with Martin. After all, there could be a perfectly rational explanation as to why the three of them were dining together. But she had an uncomfortable feeling that Amanda was up to something.

'I'm sure there's a perfectly simple explanation,' she told Scott. 'So, earlier, you were about to tell me why you wanted to go abroad.'

Scott spooned sugar into his coffee. 'Oh, I missed out on a gap year and time is marching on. I've got a few savings and I'd like to see something of the world. So how about joining me?'

Juliet swallowed. She knew she'd have to let him down gently. 'I wasn't sure if you were being serious before. Actually, Scott, I'm really enjoying being at Linden Manor. I'd like to stay there for a bit.'

He looked disappointed. 'Oh well, it was worth a try. I fancy starting off with America. I've always wanted to take a look at the Grand Canyon. Ever been there?'

Juliet shook her head. He enthused over his travel plans for a time and she realised what a restless individual he was.

'I just hope you stay around long enough to finish helping with the decorating,' she teased.

'Oh, I'm not planning to go quite yet,' he assured her with a grin. 'I need to get more funds together first, and I'll continue to live in hope that you'll change your mind and accompany me.'

Finishing their coffee they decided to go for a stroll round the grounds. As they reached a secluded spot, Scott threw an arm around Juliet's waist and drew her close. 'I really care about you, Juliet. If you came to America with me we could get to know each other better and, who knows, you might grow to care about me, too.'

He kissed her then. After a moment, she extricated herself from his embrace. 'Scott, you're a lovely guy, and I value your friendship, but I'm afraid I don't have any romantic feelings for you,' she told him gently. 'I've enjoyed this evening and your company, but now I'd like to go home.'

Scott sighed. 'I had a feeling you were going to say that. It's Martin, isn't it? I still think you're wasting your time there, and I just hope I'm around to pick up the pieces when you find out I was right.'

Juliet wasn't sure how to reply to this. She denied it but, deep down, she knew that Scott was right. She was falling for Martin even though she knew there was no future in it.

Jane Harris came into the reception area the following morning, carrying a large box of continental chocolates which she placed on the desk.

'This is for you and your colleagues,' she told Juliet with a smile. 'I've had a wonderful time.'

Thanking her, Juliet came to the front of the desk and received a hug.

'Young Josh was quite tearful when we parted company just now,' Jane told her. 'His mother was telling me he's recently lost his grandmother, and now he thinks he's losing me too. I've told him no such luck! I'm planning to be around for a while yet, and they don't live too far away from me in Cambridgeshire, so they're coming to visit one Saturday ... Ah, here's Martin!'

'Have you said all your goodbyes?' he wanted to know.

'Yes, but I'll be back soon to see how all this wonderful work is progressing,' she told Juliet.

'Then we'd better get a move on and

182

get it finished,' Martin said, and winked at Juliet, who felt sure that Jane would keep to her word and return before too long.

Juliet was glad that Martin's aunt approved of what they were doing. In the short time that the elderly lady had been at Linden Manor, Juliet had grown to like and respect her. It would be devastating if their plan to improve things didn't succeed, and the hotel was sold after all.

Martin had arranged to be away until Saturday morning. Juliet hoped she could catch up with him on his return to find out whether Carl Benfield was likely to put the kibosh on their plans.

The decorating was coming along well in the staff quarters. Bob's son-in-law had finished the ceiling and was concentrating his efforts on the guest room. On Friday morning, Juliet found Karen beavering away. Karen looked up with a smile.

'Oh, good! I was hoping you'd be free. It seems ages since we caught up for a chinwag. This is looking good already, isn't it?'

Juliet surveyed the room, hands on hips. 'Brilliant! I don't know what Martin's planning to do about the carpet, although he did say there might be another roll stashed away somewhere — probably left over from the one they used in the dining-room.'

Karen stopped for a breather. 'Oh, that would tone in well. This furniture is a bit tatty. There's plenty of self-assembly stuff about that wouldn't cost an arm and a leg.'

'We have to wait and see what the budget stretches to. Some of the ballroom fitments are in desperate need of replacing, and they won't come cheap.'

'Do you have any idea what the budget is?' Karen asked.

Juliet hesitated. 'Only for what I'm involved with. Beyond that, no. I have to run everything past either Bob or Martin.'

'Rumour has it Bob and his son-in-law are already doing up one of the guest rooms,' Karen said, looking steadily at her friend.

Juliet nodded. 'Yes, I suppose it's difficult to keep quiet about something like that. I can't really say anything at present, but all will be revealed when the time is right.'

'OK, I won't press you. Now, Iain and I are both free on Sunday and, looking at the rota, I've noticed you and Scott are off duty too — so how about the four of us meeting at mine for Sunday lunch? Rumour also has it that you went out with Scott on Wednesday evening.'

'Well, we are old friends and that's what old friends do sometimes,' Juliet said. 'But let's get one thing straight, Karen — we are not, and never will be, an item.'

Karen surveyed her friend, head on one side. 'Oh dear, have I put my foot in it? Sorry! Marina is going to be so disappointed.'

'That's a pity, but I don't intend to date Scott just to please her!' Juliet said more sharply than she intended.

'Right. Perhaps I won't invite him then.'

Juliet gave her friend an apologetic look. 'Don't mind me! I'm fond of Scott, but I don't want people getting the wrong idea about us, because there isn't any *us.* Invite him by all means. He's a good laugh and it'd be fun.'

Karen gave a sigh of relief. 'Phew! D'you know, for a minute there, I thought you two had fallen out big time.' She gave Juliet a friendly punch on the arm. 'I'd feel a bit responsible if you had — because I gave him those complimentary meal vouchers for the Country Club!'

'What?' The two of them laughed, and the awkward moment passed.

* * *

Juliet was standing near the front entrance of the hotel, having a quick word with Scott about the decorating, before going back on reception.

Scott nodded. 'Right, that sounds good and, you'll be pleased to know Martin's filled me in about your plan. Not too sure about all the secrecy, but I suppose it

186

doesn't pay to be too open when Sheldon Enterprises are sniffing around.'

Suddenly a silver Porsche swung onto the drive and, a moment or two later, a large, middle-aged man stepped out.

Scott nudged Juliet's arm. 'Isn't that …?'

Juliet nodded. 'The guy we saw with Amanda and Jamie last night. D'you reckon he knows Martin's away and has come to snoop around?'

'Possibly. I'd better go and see what he wants.'

'I've got a bad feeling about this, Scott. I've got a sneaking suspicion this isn't an altogether innocent visit. Shall I go and warn Karen?'

'Yes. Juliet, I think you know more about this guy than you're letting on.'

Carl Benfield was coming up the steps, looking purposeful.

'Don't mention we're redecorating those rooms,' she cautioned. 'I'll tell Bob and Jim to keep the doors locked, just in case.'

'This all sounds very cloak and dagger … OK, leave it to me, but I'll expect a proper explanation as to what's going on.'

Scott stepped forward to greet their guest and Juliet scooted off to Martin's office in search of Karen. If only she'd had the chance to tell Martin that they'd seen Carl Benfield at the Country Club on Wednesday evening!

'Whatever's wrong?' Karen demanded as Juliet came bursting into the room.

'Karen, I know this is going to sound weird, but you have to trust me on this one. There's a guy on the premises who's likely to ask a lot of awkward questions given half a chance, particularly about improvements, additional staffing and Martin's whereabouts. His name's Carl Benfield — you might have met him.'

Karen frowned. 'Carl Benfield you say? Oh, yes, he's frequently in touch — he's a relation of the previous owners, and still connected to the hotel in some way. I've not been able to fathom it out, and Martin can be very close. Carl seems to have quite a lot of influence still. OK Juliet, if I encounter him I'll play ignorant — refer him to Martin on every issue

... Hang on, just let me check the diary.'

Karen ran her finger down the day's entries and then double checked on the screen. 'No. As I thought, he doesn't have an appointment with Martin, so he must have just turned up hoping to catch him. Hope it's nothing serious.'

So did Juliet, after seeing him speaking with Amanda and Jamie on Wednesday evening; she was wondering what on earth his business could be. After all, Amanda must have told him his aunt was staying at Linden Manor, and he'd made no attempt to see her. Juliet hurried up the back stairs, which was the quickest route to the guest rooms. Bob and Jim were having a tea-break.

'Wow! This is looking amazing! D'you think you could keep the door well and truly locked for the time being? We've got a visitor on the premises who's probably going to be taking a look round, and we want to keep quiet about the renovations for the time being.'

'Will do, boss,' Bob saluted jovially. 'Martin told us this job was a bit special.

I bet it's that Carl Benfield come to have a nosey round whilst Martin's out of the way.'

Juliet stared at him open-mouthed. 'How on earth would you know that?'

'My missus has a sister who works at The Grange. Apparently, he's just been given the guided tour of the place. Not sure what his game is but, personally, I wouldn't trust him further than I could throw him.'

'Really? What makes you say that?' Juliet asked, hoping she could glean a bit more information.

'Oh, Bob's got a sort of sixth sense,' Jim chimed in. 'You'd never believe that chap was related to that nice Mrs Harris, would you? Now, what do you want us to do next — the fitments in the bathroom upstairs or start on this one? Got to wait for the paint to dry, you see.'

'Stay in here until Carl Benfield has gone — then you won't risk running into him and being asked any awkward questions. I'll keep you informed,' Juliet advised and hurried back downstairs again.

Carl Benfield finally left the premises around four o'clock. It seemed he'd given both Karen and Scott a thorough grilling. They had stood their ground and told him he'd have to wait for Martin's return before he could take a look at any invoices or accounts.

'He wasn't well pleased, I can tell you,' Karen said, having slipped out of the office to speak with Juliet, 'but it's not up to us, and Martin's mobile is switched off, so he must be out somewhere. I know he sends oceans of emails to Carl Benfield. Actually, I got the distinct impression our visitor knew full well that Martin had taken Mrs Harris back to Norfolk. In my opinion, he wanted to take a sneaky look round whilst Martin was out of the way. Anyway, we'll have a proper catch-up on Sunday.'

'He quizzed me too,' Juliet told her friend. 'Amongst other things, he wanted to know how long I'd worked here, what my job description was and did I like being here.'

'You didn't tell him about the interior

design work, did you?'

'Absolutely not, although he managed to wheedle out of me that I'd worked for Cramphorn's.'

Scott walked through reception just then, looking like a thundercloud.

'That man must be the world's biggest nightmare! Just wait until I catch up with Martin for landing us in it like that!'

'Be fair, Scott, Martin couldn't possibly have known Carl was going to turn up, could he now? Karen said he didn't have an appointment.'

Just then, one of the guests came to the desk to enquire about lost sunglasses, and Scott and Karen moved away.

That evening Scott was involved in organising an energetic session of line-dancing in the ballroom, and so Juliet didn't have the chance to speak with him again, although she was dying to know what had happened.

8

Martin returned half way through the following morning and was closeted in the office with Scott for a considerable length of time. With a sinking heart, Juliet wondered again if the visit from Carl Benfield had been significant.

She was just about to go on her lunch break when Martin came into reception and leant across the desk.

'Any chance of saving my sanity by having lunch with me?'

Heart racing, Juliet accepted, thinking how tired and drawn he was looking.

'I'll have to be on the terrace in case I'm needed,' he told her. 'I've sent Scott off duty for the rest of the day before he reaches melt down. OK if I get Chef to do a selection of his speciality sandwiches?'

* * *

Ten minutes later, Juliet found herself sitting opposite Martin on the terrace.

'No wonder I'm hardly ever away from the hotel,' he said. 'I go away for a couple of days and we get an unwelcome visitor.'

'Carl Benfield,' Juliet said, stating the obvious.

He nodded. 'How on earth could he have known I was away?'

'Did Scott tell you we saw him at the Country Club on Wednesday evening? I'm almost certain he and his companions didn't notice us.'

'No, Scott was far too busy telling me about Carl's visit here. I gather he put everyone through their paces ... So, who was he with on Wednesday, Juliet? Anyone you knew?'

Juliet hesitated and Martin looked at her keenly. At that moment the waitress brought their sandwiches, a wonderful selection including crab and salmon, with a colourful side salad.

'Great! I'm ravenous! Breakfast was hours ago. Tuck in!'

When they'd both got their food in

front of them, Martin fixed her with an intense gaze. 'You were about to tell me who Carl's companions were. Come on, Juliet! If there's something I should know then out with it.'

She swallowed, but knew he was bound to find out sooner or later.

'Scott recognised one of them as Jamie Parrish from The Grange and his companion was, er — Amanda Pearson.'

For a moment Martin was silent. He rested his chin on his hand and looked thoughtful.

'Amanda! I've seen her with Jamie before, but I thought they were just colleagues.'

'I'm sorry, Martin. I realise the two of you are close. Perhaps it was just a business meal and they invited Amanda along. I wanted to tell you before you went to Norfolk, but there wasn't the opportunity.'

'No, and I left my mobile behind when I took Aunt Jane to the garden centre yesterday.' He sighed. 'Carl is impossible these days, Juliet. If he had his way, we'd be selling up tomorrow.'

He bit hungrily into a sandwich. 'Karen tells me we have you to thank for your quick thinking when he arrived yesterday. She says if it hadn't been for you warning her that he was on the premises, things could have been a lot more awkward — so thank you, Juliet, yet again.'

He reached out and placed his hand over hers and her heart beat quickened.

'I was only too pleased to help and, as far as I'm aware, Carl hasn't sussed out about the refurbishments.'

'That's good, but he'd seen the advert for extra staff and questioned Karen about that. Of course, I knew I'd have to run it past him, but hoped Aunt Jane would get the chance to speak with Edwin first. Anyway, Karen coped admirably by all accounts. As my PA, she has learnt to be the very soul of discretion, but there are certain things even she doesn't know about. Scott, on the other hand, was given a hard time by Carl — and then he gave me a hard time for keeping him in the dark.'

'That was hardly fair,' she protested, but Martin raised his hand.

'No, he was right. I've been guilty of keeping too much to myself for far too long. I thought the less the staff knew about the situation the better, but now I'm beginning to realise my mistake.'

'But now you've got your Aunt Jane on your side, so surely that's good?'

He sighed wearily. 'Yes, I thought so. But, as she pointed out, she and Edwin won't be able to run the business without Carl's support. Carl's already in his fifties, and has more than one iron in the fire.'

'Surely they can find someone else,' Juliet said, selecting another of the mouth-watering sandwiches.

'If only, but I'm afraid it's not that easy, Juliet. All the time Carl thinks there's something in it for him — his future inheritance — he's going to want to protect his interests. He's not going to let someone else in on the act. Not only that — if Edwin and Jane appointed someone else in place of Carl then another set of complications would arise. Whoever it was would probably want a bigger salary than Carl is receiving. Believe you me, he knows his worth!'

Juliet couldn't conceal her disappointment. 'It's such a shame. I suppose Carl is doing everything in his power to persuade his father to sell out to Sheldon Enterprises?'

Martin nodded. 'You've got it in one. As Aunt Jane pointed out to me, she and Edwin won't be around for ever and then, in all probability, the hotel will have to be sold anyway. After all, Edwin will leave his share to Carl and his family.'

'Well, no-one can say you haven't done your best.' She pushed the plate of sandwiches towards him. 'Come on, you need to build up your strength if you're going to have to deal with Carl Benfield.'

Martin was forced to laugh. 'I suppose you don't happen to have any more bright ideas?'

She thought for a moment. 'Only if Mrs Harris happens to have any rich relations or friends who would like to buy Edwin's share of the hotel, or if you could find an investor, other than Sheldon Enterprises, who'd be prepared to run the hotel much along the same lines as its being run now, and retain its individuality.'

'Who knows? There might be a millionaire out there who's just desperate to invest in a place like this. Or, on the other hand, pigs might fly!'

Martin got to his feet as Karen appeared on the terrace and beckoned to him. 'Edwin Benfield's on the phone wanting to speak with you, Martin.'

'Goodness — he hasn't wasted any time, has he? Thanks again, Juliet, for being a good listener,' he added quietly.

Juliet sat there for a moment or two longer, staring into space, wishing she meant a bit more to him than just being a good listener or an ideas person.

Presently, Scott came into reception swinging a tennis racquet and looking hot.

'Nothing like a good game of tennis to make one unwind. Iain and I went down to the courts whilst he was waiting for Karen to have her lunch break. We saw you were having lunch with Martin. Did he bend your ear about our little *contretemps?*'

'Certainly not!' Juliet told him. 'What's said between the pair of you is none of my concern.'

Fortunately the phone rang just then and, by the time she'd finished dealing with the call, Scott had gone.

★   ★   ★

Juliet made a long phone call to her parents in Wiltshire that evening. It was good to catch up with all the latest family news.

It was almost eight-thirty when she put her mobile down. She changed into jeans and T-shirt and went downstairs again to the staff sitting-room.

Martin was watching a documentary. He looked up with a smile as she sat down. 'Fancy coming for a walk? Scott's volunteered to hold the fort for an hour or so, as he's got tomorrow off. I gather you're all going to Karen's.'

'Yes, she's invited us for lunch. Yes please, I quite fancy a leg stretch. Where were you thinking of going?'

He consulted his watch. 'How about I show you where my grandparents used to live? We've just about got time. And I can tell you a piece of interesting news at the same time.'

Intrigued, Juliet followed him along the drive. Half way down, they took a short cut along a footpath, which petered out suddenly by the boundary of the grounds. All Juliet could see was a hedge. Puzzled, she looked at Martin.

'There's a wicket gate further along — see!' He fished in his pocket and found the key to the padlock. The gate creaked protestingly as they emerged into a narrow lane.

'I've never been this far!' Juliet exclaimed. 'I've always gone in the opposite direction towards the village.'

'I don't invite everyone on my secret walks,' he told her with a little smile.

As they rounded a bend in the lane, they came upon a row of ragstone cottages. 'My grandparents lived in the last one. They've all been sold now, but at one time they belonged to the estate, together with the lodge near the drive.'

The end cottage had a small front garden which was a blaze of colour. There were spotless white net curtains at the windows, and a trellis arch with roses climbing up it near the front door. Martin stood for a few moments lost in thought, and Juliet left him to his reverie.

'I had some good times here when I was a youngster,' he said presently. 'There's a stream running through the gardens at the back. Great for paddling in! Those were the days … Memories, eh!'

'Thanks for sharing them with me. It's such a pretty cottage. What became of your grandparents?'

'Oh, they both died a few years ago, within a few months of each other,' he said sadly. 'Marina knew them years back — says there's a lot of my grandfather in me.'

They stood looking at the cottages for a few minutes longer.

'Come on, let's get back through that gate, before it gets dark,' he said suddenly.

On an impulse Juliet caught hold of his arm, and they wandered back along the lane. 'So, what's this interesting news you were going to tell me? Was it to do with that phone call from Edwin Benfield at lunch time?'

'Got it in one! I can't tell you everything we talked about, but you'll be pleased to know Aunt Jane managed to speak to Edwin before Carl bent his ear. Edwin is prepared to let us forge ahead with the refurbishment — has even agreed to pay towards the cost. Jane has convinced him it's in his best interest. He's coming to take a look shortly.'

'Wow, so we've got him on our side too!'

'Not entirely, I'm afraid, but it's certainly a start. Edwin's still considering selling his share of the hotel but realises that unless Aunt Jane agrees to sell her share too there can be no deal with Sheldon Enterprises. Anyway, we've got a reprieve for a while whilst we find that millionaire!'

Juliet laughed. 'And have you discovered why Carl Benfield was dining with Jamie and Amanda?'

'No, I'm still trying to fathom that one out. I might challenge Carl about it — without mentioning you and Scott, of course.'

'Actually,' Juliet said slowly, 'I've just remembered something Scott told me. He mentioned Jamie was related to the manager of The Grange.'

Martin stared at her. 'Really! I wasn't aware of that. Perhaps that's the answer. You see, the manager, Bryan Heath, has a brother who married into the Sheldon family.'

Juliet frowned. 'How does that …? Oh, I see. Carl's trying to find out just how interested Sheldon Enterprises would be in purchasing Linden Manor Hotel.'

'My goodness, Miss Marple, you're missing your vocation,' he teased.

They reached the gate and went back into the grounds of the hotel. Martin secured the padlock again.

'Carl isn't going to be pleased when he

learns that both his father and Aunt Jane might not be prepared to sell up after all, although unfortunately, he can be very persuasive. There's a bit more, but I'm not in a position to tell you at present … Anyway, enough of all that for now. There's an Alan Ayckbourn play on at the village hall next week. If I can manoeuvre my off duty times, would you like to come with me?'

'That would be fantastic,' she told him, pulse racing, 'but, what about Amanda? Wouldn't you prefer …?'

He took her hands between his. 'Juliet, I'm asking you to accompany me — unless you'd rather go with Scott.'

'Scott? Oh, I don't think plays are his thing and anyway …'

He was looking at her intently and she mumbled. 'He's got a couple of days off next week and he's going to see his family.'

Juliet wished she could come right out with it and tell Martin that, so far as she was concerned, Scott would only ever be a good friend. But then she thought of Amanda, and decided it was probably best to leave things as they were.

She puzzled as to why Amanda would invite Martin to her parents' Spanish villa if she was involved with Jamie Parrish. But if it had just been a business dinner with Carl at the Country Club, then why was Amanda involved?

'Here we are again,' Martin said lightly as they arrived back at Linden Manor. 'I feel much better for that walk.'

'So do I,' Juliet assured him. 'Thanks for suggesting it, Martin. And I'll look forward to the play next week.'

'So will I.' He gave her a gentle kiss on the cheek, making her heartbeat quicken. Juliet's emotions were in turmoil as they entered the hotel and went their separate ways.

★　★　★

The following afternoon, replete after Karen's roast chicken lunch, the four friends sat in the pretty little garden and discussed Carl Benfield's visit.

'I felt as though I'd been put through one of those old-fashioned mangles my Great Nan used to tell me about — thoroughly wrung out,' Karen admitted.

'Ditto!' Scott agreed. 'What a thoroughly unpleasant man!'

'Martin was very pleased with the way everyone handled the situation,' Karen told him. 'Hopefully, we won't be left to deal with things if he turns up again.'

Scott pulled a face. 'If I see that guy coming up the drive, I'll barricade myself in my room until he's gone. I'd still like to know what he was doing at the Country Club with Amanda and Jamie.'

'Wouldn't we all,' Karen said brightly. 'Now, who's for one of these gorgeous chocolates Iain bought me — and it isn't even my birthday!'

'How long d'you think it will take to finish the refurbishment, Juliet?' Iain asked, as he chewed on a hazelnut whirl.

'One of the staff bed-sits is virtually ready now. Marina's working flat out on the curtains and I've just got to finish upholstering an armchair. Bob's going to lay the carpet as soon as he finds time. Then we can get cracking on the second room.'

'Has Martin had any response to the advert for new staff?' Scott wanted to know.

'Oh, there've been one or two enquiries. These things take time,' Karen said carefully.

'And what about the new guest rooms?' Iain wanted to know.

'The one that's being worked on is looking wonderful,' Juliet told him, deciding there was no longer any need for secrecy, 'but there's still a lot to do.'

'It'll get done,' Karen said, 'and now, can we please change the subject? Much as I enjoy my job, there are other things besides work, you know.'

'Are there?' Iain asked in mock amazement. 'Such as?'

The other three groaned and Karen nudged him sharply in the ribs so that he nearly fell off the flimsy garden chair. There were gales of laughter as he righted himself.

'That's brilliant!' Martin said, looking with admiration at the new staff bed-sitter.

Juliet smiled at him. 'Not bad, is it? All we need now is someone to put in it.'

'Oh, we've had several applications, and I'm putting together a short list.'

He bent to examine the armchair Juliet was re-covering. 'I like this fabric. You've got a real flair for this, Juliet.'

'Just you wait till you see the guest room. Bob and Jim have worked like slaves and now all that's needed are the new carpet and curtains. They're starting on one of the other guest rooms this week.'

Martin put a hand on her shoulder making her pulse race. 'I've got another piece of good news to tell you.'

She stared at him. 'What's that?'

'I've been given the go-ahead to refurbish another two guest rooms in addition to those, *and* another staff bed-sit. How's that for progress?'

'Wow! How did that come about?'

'Aunt Jane was so impressed with what she saw, and with our work ethic, that she's somehow managed to convince Edwin that investment is the way forward — the only way to put Linden Manor on the map.'

'And it will work,' Juliet assured him, eyes alight with enthusiasm. 'We're already taking bookings for next year. Just think — with an extra four rooms we'll be able to accommodate up to eight more guests for starters.'

'Carl's not best pleased,' Martin told her. 'I had an extremely difficult phone conversation with him. I won't repeat what he said, but he obviously blames me for a number of things.'

'He's clearly keen to sell the hotel. Did you happen to mention he'd been spotted with Amanda and Jamie?'

Martin hesitated. 'Actually, no — thought better of it. It doesn't always do to give too much away. No doubt, all will be revealed in due course. Now, about our theatre trip tomorrow — shall we make arrangements now?'

They had just settled on a time to meet up when Amanda Pearson appeared in the doorway, looking glamorous and waving a beach bag.

'So this is where you're hiding, Martin. Karen said you'd be up here somewhere. I thought we could go for a swim before our meeting.'

Martin looked awkward. 'Nice idea Amanda, but I've got rather a tight schedule. The craft fayre is next week so there's a lot to do.'

Amanda pouted and caught his arm. 'Oh, come on, you need to chill out. What's the point of having a swimming pool here if you never get to use it?'

'It's tempting,' he agreed. 'OK, give me ten minutes to sign a few letters Karen wants to get in the post today.'

Amanda cast a critical eye over the bed-sitter. 'This is an improvement on when I last saw the staff quarters. Although I can't say I like the colour scheme — bit too traditional for my taste.'

'It's just as well you don't have to live

here then,' Juliet remarked, inwardly seething.

Amanda chose to ignore her. 'I saw the advert for new staff. Hadn't realised anyone was leaving.'

'No, we just need some additional staff,' Martin replied briefly.

Amanda gave Juliet a curious look. 'Really? I thought you were helping Layla on reception these days. Have you had a switch round? I noticed Kirsty was on the desk just now.'

'Kirsty is covering for Juliet, to enable her to do some interior design work,' Martin explained.

Amanda's face was a picture. Carl Benfield clearly hadn't filled her in on this yet. 'Are you telling me that those old skinflints have coughed up at last? I got the distinct impression they were happy to let this place fall into a crumbling pile.'

'You have a fertile imagination,' Martin told her with a smile. 'Why would they want to do that when it's going from strength to strength?'

Amanda looked a little uncertain and

then laughed. 'You're winding me up, aren't you, Martin? Everyone knows the owners, whoever they might be, have little interest in this place.'

'Then everyone knows differently from me,' Martin told her. 'Now, are we going for that swim or not?'

Amanda hooked her arm in Martin's and, as they stepped into the corridor, turned back to glance at Juliet, a triumphant look on her face.

Juliet shut the door and sank onto the bed, wondering just what game Amanda was playing. It was obvious she knew how to sweet talk Martin. Juliet sighed. He didn't seem to notice her when Amanda was around. She thought back to the swim they had enjoyed such a short time ago.

She got to her feet, pulling herself together with an effort. There was still the theatre trip to look forward to the following evening. She was determined to enjoy every moment she spent with Martin, and not let Amanda spoil things for her.

⋆ ⋆ ⋆

'I'm looking forward to the craft fayre,' Layla informed Juliet. 'We had one last year and it was a great success. It's quite widely advertised and should bring in quite a few people who might help our profile.'

'Really? Such as?' Juliet asked with interest.

'One or two journalists, for starters.'

Remembering her first encounter with Martin, Juliet began to laugh and then had to explain to a mystified Layla what had amused her. Layla saw the funny side of it too.

'My mother loves craft fayres,' Juliet told her friend, when they'd both sobered down.

'Why don't you ask her along?' Layla suggested.

'Nice idea, but my parents live rather a long way away.' Juliet considered. 'I suppose they could always stay here and try out the new guest room. They wouldn't

214

mind if it wasn't quite finished.'

'That's a great idea, and you'd get a good staff discount ... Of course, events like this are hard work. Amanda and Martin put their heads together to plan it all out. The other two hotels send us some of their staff to help out on these occasions.'

'That's one way of doing things, I suppose,' Juliet conceded. 'And I guess they'll just happen to promote their hotels at the same time?'

'Obviously. Some of the traders stay overnight and opt to stay in one of the other hotels. We couldn't accommodate them all here. And then you get the craft fayre-mad members of the public who follow these events round the country and fit their holidays around them. When we run out of space the other hotels accommodate them, too. Pity we haven't got more rooms available.'

'But, we will have before long — once the work's finished on the new ones,' Juliet pointed out.

Just then one of the guests appeared

in a bit of a panic. 'I've left my handbag inside my room and my husband's gone for a walk and taken the key.'

'Not to worry,' Juliet reassured her. 'I'll get the master key and we'll have your room open in a jiffy.'

Mrs Towner was a chatty little lady and, once she'd rescued her bag, kept Juliet talking for several minutes. 'I was saying to that blonde-haired girl who arranges all the events, what a lovely place this is. She said she was doing some sort of survey — asked me and my husband all sorts of questions. Anyway, we told her we can't fault this place. It's just what we needed, a bit of peace and quiet. My husband's had a lot of stress recently — been made redundant.'

Juliet made the appropriate noises while her mind was working overtime. She had no knowledge of any survey being circulated. She would ask Karen. She popped into the office on her way back to reception.

Karen frowned. 'Survey? First I've heard of it. Leave it with me, and I'll do some investigating. Both Martin and Scott are tied up at present — trying to sort out last minute matters for next week. Between you and me, I wouldn't put anything past Amanda. She's probably been asked to suss things out by Carl Benfield.'

'But why? What can she possibly have to gain from it?'

'No idea, but I wouldn't trust her further than I can throw her. She was busy showing off her tan by the pool yesterday — to say nothing of her designer swimwear, what little there was of it!'

'She and Martin had a swim together before their meeting,' Juliet told her, trying to sound as if she didn't care. 'I'd best get back or Layla will think I've done a runner.'

★　★　★

The village hall was packed that evening. The local Amateur Dramatic Society was very popular and their producer was a retired professional actor.

There wasn't much space between the chairs, which locked together, and Juliet was very conscious of Martin sitting beside her. He turned to smile at her and her heart missed a beat. Dressed casually in an electric-blue open-necked shirt, and darker blue trousers, she thought he was devastatingly good-looking.

'It looks like the entire village has turned out to support them. It seems like it's going to be a good evening.'

Juliet smiled back just as the lights dimmed and the play began. She thoroughly enjoyed the production of *A Small Family Business*. There was a lot of talent amongst the cast and the audience was appreciative.

'What d'you think?' Martin asked as they queued for coffee during the interval.

'Oh, it's superb. I do so enjoy Alan Ayckbourn. I got hooked on his plays when I was a teenager and my family and I were staying in Scarborough. My father's a great fan of his and took us along to the theatre. Thanks for inviting me, Martin.'

'My pleasure. I enjoy your company.' He gave her arm a gentle squeeze. 'Anyway, how could I resist coming to see a play with such an apt title?'

Juliet puzzled over this. 'Oh, you mean because of our situation at Linden Manor?'

He winked at her and she laughed.

'Did you notice several of our guests are here tonight?' he asked as they sat enjoying their coffee. 'Scott's obviously done a good job of procuring tickets and organising transport.'

She was tempted to ask if that wasn't supposed to be Amanda's job, but instead said, 'Yes, he certainly deserves his days off. Actually Martin, I meant to ask you. My mother's mad keen on craft fayres. It's their wedding anniversary this weekend, and Dad's arranged one of those theatre and dinner trips as a surprise. He's sure she'd love to come on here afterwards, and I was wondering if they could stay in the new guest room for a night or two. I know it's not quite finished, but they wouldn't mind that.'

'Absolutely — that's a great idea. I'd be

glad of some feedback. Of course, staff rates apply. Just tell the booking clerk, will you?'

'Great. Thanks. I know they're really keen to see where I'm working and to meet my colleagues. I'll ring Dad tomorrow.'

'You're fortunate to have a family who care what you're doing, Juliet,' he said wistfully, and her heart went out to him.

'Hasn't your father ever come to visit you at the hotel?'

Martin shook his head. 'We occasionally meet up in London for a meal. He enjoys travelling; the last I heard, he'd gone off on one of those adventure holidays to some far flung place whose name evades me.'

'I've got an uncle who periodically goes off on one of those trips, usually for two or three months at a stretch, and then he surfaces again ... Anyway, you'll be looking forward to a relaxing holiday in Spain soon,' she said, daringly.

The expression on Martin's face told her she'd spoken out of turn, and she wished she could retract the remark.

'So, what makes you think I've accepted the invitation?' he asked coolly.

'I assumed ...' she stammered uncomfortably.

'Then you've assumed wrongly,' he told her abruptly. 'I've no intention of going to Spain with Amanda or anyone else, at present. There's far too much going on at Linden Manor for me to take any leave.'

Just then, much to Juliet's relief, people began to take their seats ready for the next act. She wondered if Martin was just making an excuse. Perhaps he'd changed his mind about the holiday since he'd learnt about Amanda dining with Jamie and Carl Benfield. Juliet hardly dared to hope that Martin hadn't had any intention of accompanying the Events Manager to Spain in the first place.

Juliet spent the next few minutes dreaming of what it would be like to go to Spain with Martin, and then the curtain rose and she became absorbed in the play once more.

Martin suggested they went for a drink before returning to the hotel. He took her arm as they walked the short distance to the picturesque old inn.

It was a mild evening and they took their drinks outside. They discussed the play, and then talked about other productions they'd seen. Martin was very much on her wavelength, Juliet decided. She wished the evening could go on forever but, all too soon, it was time to leave.

Outside the inn they encountered a couple of guests staying at Linden Manor Hotel, and chatted with them for a few minutes.

'Hopefully, we answered all the questions for that survey properly,' the elderly man said. 'That blonde girl made out it was of great importance.'

'Well, we've done our best,' his wife added, 'although some of them were a bit difficult to fathom out. We wanted to say the right thing, because we really like Linden Manor, don't we, Alf?'

Her husband nodded. 'Been coming there for years. You're not closing, are you?'

'Absolutely not! We're actually going to be opening up one or two more guest rooms,' Martin assured them. 'Now, don't you worry about that survey. It really wasn't that important. Actually — just between you and me — it was a mistake. Just an over-enthusiastic member of staff trying out an idea that hadn't been generally agreed upon.'

The elderly couple looked relieved. So that was how Martin was playing it. Juliet kept quiet until she got into the car.

'What's all that business about the survey?' she asked directly. 'Several people have been asking me and I've referred them to Scott, but he doesn't seem to be any the wiser, either.

Martin shook his head and looked impatient. 'I've sorted it,' he told her in a dismissive tone. 'As I've just said, it was all a mistake — end of story!'

And Juliet had to be content with that.

'Right. So, let's hope that really is the end of it,' she said, wishing that they hadn't met up with the elderly guests. Up until then it had been a lovely evening, but now Martin seemed withdrawn and occupied with his own thoughts.

She wondered what had passed between him and Amanda regarding that survey. That young woman had a lot to answer for, so far as Juliet was concerned.

Martin pulled up just before they reached the hotel and, reaching over, took Juliet's hands in his. 'Thanks for a lovely evening.'

'That was my line,' she told him. 'I've really enjoyed it.'

'Then perhaps we could do it again sometime.'

'A repeat performance?' she asked teasingly.

'Or even an encore,' he said, leaning towards her. Juliet closed her eyes as his lips encountered her. The kiss was beyond her wildest dreams.

9

Craft fayre fever took over the hotel for the next few days. It was manic. Juliet was still on a high from her evening out with Martin, but had to content herself with just catching an occasional glimpse of him as he dashed about the place.

'Is it always like this?' she asked Karen as they snatched a hurried lunch together.

'Well, I wasn't here this time last year, of course, but from what everyone tells me it's quite normal. Once everything's up and running I'm sure it'll be fantastic ...'

'When do your parents arrive?'

'Tomorrow — late afternoon. They're off to Herts in the morning to see some friends and pick up the rest of my stuff from Janet's. I expect she'll be pleased to get rid of it.'

Karen surveyed her friend, head on one side. 'You're looking happy, Juliet — radiant in fact. Is there something you're not telling me? Is it to do with you and Scott? You seemed to be getting on really well when you came to lunch.'

Juliet felt the colour rise to her cheeks. 'I don't know what you mean, Karen. I've already told you, Scott and I have got a good relationship and ...'

She trailed off as Karen said, 'Hello Martin — did you want me or Juliet?'

'You, but finish your lunch first. I'll be in the office.'

Glancing up, Juliet saw Martin standing beside Karen's chair, hands in pockets. He didn't look in her direction, making her feel as if she'd suddenly become invisible. A moment later he was gone, leaving Juliet miserably wondering just how much of their conversation he'd overheard. Now he was bound to get the wrong impression of her relationship with Scott all over again.

She drank her orange juice, trying to compose herself — not wanting Karen to notice that there was anything amiss.

'That man's on the go from dawn to dusk,' Karen commented, getting to her feet and brushing the crumbs from her trousers. 'I wonder what he wants now. Let's hope nothing else has gone wrong. Sorry, Juliet. We're going to have to finish our conversation another time. See you later.'

Juliet screwed her napkin into a ball and pushed her plate to one side, having suddenly lost her appetite. If only Martin hadn't turned up when he had. She had been about to reiterate that, whilst she got on fine with Scott, there was absolutely no question of them being anything other than good friends. She sighed and little Mrs Towner, passing the table, stopped in her tracks.

'Are you all right, dear? You look as if you've got the weight of the world on your shoulders.'

Juliet was tempted to reply that she had, but instead, forced herself to smile. 'Oh, I'm fine thank you, Mrs Towner. We're just extra busy at the moment with the craft fayre looming.'

Mrs Towner wanted to chat. 'Let's hope this craft fayre is a big success. I'm really looking forward to it — hoping to buy some Christmas presents.'

'Christmas presents!' Juliet echoed.

'Yes, dear, I know it's only summer but the time will just fly by, and I always say you can never start shopping too early for Christmas. Besides, we might have to tighten our belts if Stan doesn't find himself a part-time job soon, so we might as well spend it whilst we've got it, eh!'

She paused for breath and Juliet made to move away, but Mrs Towner put a detaining hand on her shoulder. 'There's a rumour going round that the hotel's in financial straits. What with the recession and everything, I suppose lots of businesses like this are noticing the pinch.'

'Where did you hear this, er, rumour?' Juliet asked, momentarily distracted from her thoughts of Martin.

Mrs Towner frowned in concentration. 'D'you know, I can't quite remember. It was probably when we were sitting by the pool the other day. We're having such a good time here, I'd hate to think it was true.'

'It isn't,' Juliet assured her decisively. 'I have absolutely no idea how these rumours get started, but you can take my word for it — there's absolutely no truth in that one. So if you hear anyone else saying that, then scotch it, please, and you'll be doing us all a big favour.'

Little Mrs Towner drew herself up to her full height, raised her arm and clenched her fist comically. 'I'll tell them I've got it on the best authority it's not true — so they can just stop talking a lot of silly nonsense!'

Juliet had to smile and, seizing her moment, made her escape with a cheery wave that didn't match her mood. There was one consolation she told herself as she returned to reception. If the hotel was sold and a whole lot of new staff was recruited, then she wouldn't have to stay and watch Amanda making sheep's eyes at Martin.

'Have you heard any more about the interviews for the new members of staff?' Layla enquired as she prepared to go off duty.

'Yes, apparently they're being held as

soon as this craft fayre is out of the way,' Juliet told her, as she returned some keys to the board behind her.

Layla popped a couple of pens into a holder on the desk. 'D'you suppose that dreadful Carl Benfield will be there — now that he's started making his presence felt about the place?'

'I hope not!' Juliet said with feeling. 'He might take it into his head to start cross-examining everyone again. Apparently, he had one of the catering staff in tears. The poor girl was so nervous that she dropped a dish of vegetables right in front of him, and he ended up with a dollop of mashed potato on his expensive shoe!'

'If it had been me, I'd have dropped one on his other shoe so that he had a matching pair of pompoms,' Layla said wickedly.

They were still laughing when Amanda Pearson appeared at the desk, blonde hair immaculate, uniform pristine.

'When you two have quite finished, perhaps you can tell me where Martin is?

His mobile's switched off.'

'He could be anywhere with the craft fayre beginning tomorrow. Everyone's rushed off their feet,' Layla informed her.

Amanda raised her pencilled eyebrows. 'Then find him for me, will you — now! I haven't got all day, unlike some people. You two don't seem to be doing very much.'

Layla gasped. 'That's because you've just happened along during a lull. It's been manic all the morning … and now, if you'll excuse me, I'm just off for a late lunch.'

Amanda waited impatiently whilst Juliet tried to locate Martin. She finally unearthed him in the ballroom.

'He's in the ballroom, Amanda, if you'd care to go along there now.'

Amanda continued to stand in front of the desk. 'Before I do, I want to give you a word of warning.'

Juliet gaped at her. 'Whatever about? Have we got a dangerous animal on the loose or an escaped criminal in the area?'

Amanda's pale blue eyes narrowed.

'Don't get clever with me! It doesn't do to meddle in affairs that don't concern you. I'd watch my step around here, if I were you. That's if you want to hang onto your job! Martin and I go back a long way. We're extremely close friends — so don't go getting any ideas about coming between us, because it won't work.

'Martin's a kind-hearted guy and he's taken you out a couple of times because he feels sorry for you. Oh, yes, I know you were at that amateur do at the village hall last week! But it's me he listens to — just remember that!'

Stunned, Juliet was saved from replying by the arrival of some new guests. Before departing, Amanda shot Juliet a look that spoke volumes.

Juliet was so busy for the next half hour that she didn't have time to dwell on what Amanda had meant by her cryptic comments. When she came up for a breather, she decided that the other girl was just showing herself in her true colours, and was probably peeved because Martin was too busy to take much notice of her.

The first day of the craft fayre was still going with a swing when Juliet's parents arrived. Layla had arranged to hold the fort for half an hour whilst Juliet showed them to their room and had a bit of catch-up time.

'This is gorgeous!' Alison Croft said, surveying the newly finished guest room. 'And is it all down to you, Julie?'

'Oh, I can't take the credit for all of it, Mum, there've been a number of people involved, but the initial ideas were mine. Actually, there are one or two things still to be done, but it's not so bad, is it?'

Her father put a hand on her shoulder. 'You've done a great job. Well done, love.'

He crossed to the window. 'What a splendid view. I'd no idea this place would be so grand. I can quite understand why you like being here.'

'Oh, it's not just because of the place itself, although that's part of it. I enjoy the atmosphere and the majority of my colleagues are delightful to work with.'

'Didn't you tell us Scott Norris is the assistant manager?' her mother enquired. 'I seem to remember you were quite friendly with him when you were at Cramphorn's.'

'I was quite friendly with several people,' Juliet reminded her mother, and quickly changed the subject. 'So, did you manage to pick up the rest of my stuff from Janet's?'

'We certainly did. It's still in the boot. Didn't think you'd want us to bring it into reception,' her father joked.

'No way! We do have to maintain some standards, you know! Now, tell me about Sarah, Matt and the twins and then I must get back to reception.'

They were just on the point of leaving the room in search of some much needed refreshments when Martin appeared. He stretched out his hand to Juliet's mother.

'Hello, I'm Martin Glover, the hotel manager. Sorry, I wasn't around to welcome you when you arrived, but I see Juliet's taking care of you.'

Juliet stood to one side as Martin chatted to her parents. He was absolutely charming, and she wished she could wipe out that disastrous conversation he'd overheard between herself and Karen. She'd had a restless night mulling over what Amanda had said, trying to convince herself that there was no truth in it. Martin's kiss had set her on fire, but he obviously hadn't felt the same way. How naïve could she be?

'We were admiring the room,' her mother told Martin now. 'My daughter is in her element when it comes to doing things up.'

Martin smiled at Juliet, and suddenly all was right with her world. 'Your daughter is very talented, Mrs Croft, and we appreciate her input ... Now, how about some tea? Juliet, Scott's manning the desk for a while, so why don't you take your parents into the lounge and join them?'

'What a delightful young man,' Mrs Croft commented, as soon as he was out of earshot. 'Is he your boss, Julie?'

'Well, I have to answer to him because

the owners are elderly and mostly leave him in charge. It's a complicated set-up.' She didn't want to mention Carl Benfield and the problems they'd been experiencing recently.

'Hmm,' her father commented. 'I've heard of a care home where they've put in a manager and the owner just turns up periodically. Of course, with the internet, everything's so different nowadays. Call me old-fashioned, but I prefer the personal touch myself.'

'I, er, think Martin goes to meetings with one of the owners' representatives,' Juliet ventured, although she wasn't too sure how things were arranged. Karen had implied that Martin met up with Carl Benfield from time to time, to keep him up to date. She assumed it was probably a working lunch away from the hotel.

Fortunately, their tea arrived just then, and the conversation turned to Juliet's parents' trip to London which they had both immensely enjoyed. It was good to have them around, even if it was for such a short time.

'I'm really looking forward to looking round the craft fayre tomorrow,' her mother told her. 'It's not really your father's thing. I suppose there isn't any chance of you having any off duty, Julie?'

Juliet shook her head. 'Sorry, no — it's such a busy week. I'm supposed to have a couple of hours between shifts in the afternoon, but that's only if I can be spared.'

'Oh, I'm sure we'll find plenty to do,' her mother said, trying to hide her disappointment, 'and if not, we'll just have to keep popping back to reception with a trumped up excuse to speak to you.'

The situation resolved itself unexpectedly that evening when Martin came to speak to Juliet on reception. 'Juliet, I've had to pull Bob off the refurbishment work for the rest of the week, because he keeps being called away to do things elsewhere. So, how d'you feel about changing your work schedule? Just for this week, of course.'

'That's fine. What would you like me to do?'

'Brilliant. Well, during these events, Karen usually wanders round the stalls and does a front of house routine to make sure everything's running smoothly. I can't spare her for the whole time — too much going on behind the scenes — so, how would it be if you took over from her for a couple of hours or so each day?'

Juliet smiled broadly. 'Absolutely, I'd love to, although I haven't actually done anything like that before! I'll certainly do my best, though.'

His green eyes met her hazel ones in an intense gaze. 'I don't doubt that for one moment, Juliet, or I wouldn't be asking you. Karen will fill you in. It's quite a pleasant job, and you'll be able to spend some time with your parents when you're outside or in the ballroom. It was good to meet them earlier.'

'That would be great, Martin. I'll look forward to it,' she assured him, eyes shining.

He smiled back. 'Good, that was easily sorted … Hello, Scott, how's it going?'

Scott raised his eyes skywards.

'Wouldn't you think that having been subjected to craft fayre mania for most of the day, everyone would be ready for a change? But, no! Apparently, that large, rather dippy lady, Megan, who makes those lovely scarves, also runs courses at her local Adult Education Centre. So, she's offered to give a talk this evening ...'

Seeing the expression on Martin's face, Scott trailed off and then assured him, 'It's OK, Martin, keep your hair on! She's volunteered so there's no payment involved, although I've promised her some complimentary meal vouchers as a good-will gesture.'

Martin frowned. 'Complimentary meal vouchers! What are you talking about? We don't have any.'

'I know that, you know that, but she doesn't. I'll print a couple off and perhaps we can keep it in mind as an idea for the future.'

Martin looked about to explode. 'And you didn't think to run this past me first?'

Scott sighed. 'Martin, if this hotel is going to survive and become a thriving business, then we've got to start thinking outside of the box. Right, I'll be in the small lounge listening to Megan's talk at eight-fifteen, should you need me.'

He turned to Juliet. 'Before I forget, Juliet, your mother's opted to go to the talk, but your father's teamed up with another craft fayre widower and is going off for a stroll — they asked me to let you know. It was great to meet up with them again.'

Juliet nodded, embarrassed that she'd witnessed the exchange between Martin and Scott. Not for the first time, she realised that the two men were very different people. Scott was inclined to act on impulse and didn't always think things through. She knew that Martin was under a lot of pressure from the top management, namely Carl Benfield, and often found his hands tied when it came to making any changes.

Scott wandered off in the direction of the small lounge, whistling to himself, but Martin remained by the desk, looking awkward.

'Sorry about that — Scott takes too much upon himself sometimes.'

She smiled. 'Whilst you tend to err on the side of caution.'

He looked downcast. 'I can't do much else until I'm sure that we're out of the woods.'

She felt a wave of sympathy for him. He was so conscientious and dependable and she wondered if the Benfields were really aware of his worth.

'Well, the craft fayre's taken off with a big bang, so that's got to be good,' she said.

He brightened up. 'Yes, we've had a record number of people today, despite that slight shower this afternoon. There are quite a few more stalls than last year, and everyone I've spoken with sounded enthusiastic.'

'So, there you are then. My mother's really looking forward to wandering round tomorrow *and* Marina Norris is coming with a couple of friends.'

'Marina's a real find. Those curtains and cushion covers are really professional.'

'As good as Sheldon's?' Juliet asked teasingly.

'Equally.' He leant across the desk. 'Juliet, you're a real find too. I want you to know how much I value the work you're doing here.' He hesitated and then added quietly, 'I hope Scott's aware of just how lucky he is.'

'I'm not sure I know what you mean,' Juliet told him, desperate to put the situation right.

Martin gave her a searching glance. 'Oh, I think you do, Juliet — only too well. Scott and you are obviously ...'

He broke off again as the phone rang shrilly. When she looked up from answering it, he'd gone, and she'd missed her opportunity again. She caught her breath as she realised why it mattered so much to her to put things right between them; she'd fallen in love with Martin Glover!

Juliet spent the rest of her shift rehearsing in her head what she would say to him, if and when she ever got the chance.

10

The following morning, Juliet thoroughly enjoyed being *front of house*, as Martin called it. After a short briefing session with Karen she wandered round the stalls in the sunshine with her mother, chatting to the visitors and checking that everything was going well. It was thoughtful of Martin to have come up with this idea — she could now spend more time with her parents.

'I'm glad you're happy in your work, dear,' her mother said, as they paused at a jewellery stall. 'I know your heart is really in the interior design side of things, but it isn't always possible to follow your dreams.'

'No, I'm beginning to realise that,' Juliet said, stopping to examine a pair of amber earrings. She exchanged a few words with the woman who had designed the jewellery.

'Your father and I are relieved that you didn't accept Duncan's proposal,' Alison Croft said as they walked across the grass to take a look at Megan's scarves. 'He's a lovely guy, but apart from interior design, you didn't appear to have much in common.'

'No, he was a bit of a workaholic. At that time, Cramphorn's was my world but now that I'm in a different one ... hey, I'm beginning to realise there are other things in life besides interior design.'

'Good, because you did seem to bury yourself in your work, rather, after Evan. Your father and I had an anxious time when you told us about Duncan. It isn't a good idea to get married on the rebound.'

'Oh, you don't need to worry, Mum. There's absolutely no chance of that happening. If and when I get married, it will be to someone I truly love,' Juliet assured her.

There was a lump in her throat as she spoke these words; the one man she felt she could give her heart to was Martin, but he was still involved with Amanda, and he was convinced she was involved with Scott! She sighed and her mother looked at her in concern.

'Oh, Juliet, you're not still pining for Evan, are you?'

'No, Mum, absolutely not. Looking back, that was a big mistake. I think I had a lucky escape. Don't worry, I'm perfectly happy with the way things are.'

Her mother didn't reply. She was not at all sure that Juliet was telling her everything but then, in her experience, daughters always had their secrets.

Megan's scarves were all so beautiful and individual that it was difficult to decide which ones they liked best. They stood admiring the sea of pastel colours, swaying gently as the breeze caught hold of them.

'Your father has told me to buy three — one for each of you girls and one for me,' Alison said. 'I just love those subtle shades, but I really don't know which one to choose for myself and Sarah. What about you, Julie?'

'It's not easy,' Juliet said, first holding

up a silvery grey scarf with a delicate seashell design, and then a dainty pink one.

'Oh dear, shall we walk round and have a think about it?' her mother suggested.

'Don't think for too long,' Megan advised. 'Each one is individual so I wouldn't like you to be disappointed. I sold no end yesterday. Have you seen these?'

She pointed out another stand at the back of the stall displaying a range of more vibrant colours: oranges, purples, reds and golds. In the end they selected four scarves, and Megan carefully wrapped them up.

'I love coming here but they tell me this Fayre will probably be held elsewhere next year, at some venue in Sussex.'

Juliet stared at Megan. 'Whoever told you that has been badly misinformed.'

Megan looked uncertain for a moment. 'I don't think so, dear. They said they'd been talking to one of the owners and it's on the cards that this hotel's being sold.'

Juliet shook her head and said firmly,

'That's just a rumour that someone's put about. I can tell you there's definitely no substance in it.'

Seeing that Megan still looked doubtful she asked, 'I suppose you don't happen to know the name of the person who told you all this?'

Megan shook her head. 'I've heard it from more than one source, and have you seen those leaflets?'

Juliet frowned. 'Sorry, you've lost me — which leaflets?'

Megan rummaged in her pocket and unearthed a crumpled piece of paper. Juliet flattened out the flyer and gasped as she read it. 'Where did this come from?'

'There're a stack of them lying about and I just happened to pick one up. You can keep it if you like.'

'Thanks, I will.' Juliet was finding it hard to hide her concern. She was going to have to speak with Martin as soon as possible. She felt sure he would have told her if he were aware of any adverse publicity.

As soon as they'd moved out of earshot,

her mother asked, 'Whatever's wrong, Julie? It's to do with that piece of paper, isn't it?'

Juliet made light of the matter. 'Absolutely nothing to worry about, Mum. Just someone trying to drum up business for their own hotel at the expense of this one. People make their own choices as to where they want to stay. Actually, I'm finding it a bit hot out here, aren't you? How about us going inside for a spell? I need to check that everything's OK in the ballroom, anyway.'

They stopped to look at a couple more stalls en route, and Mrs Croft purchased a leather spectacle case for her husband and a gemstone necklace for Juliet's cousin, who had a birthday coming up.

Juliet saw Scott chatting to some people by the ballroom door. She wondered if she should show him the flyer, but decided he'd probably seen it already. No, she would wait until Karen arrived to take over from her and then go in search of Martin.

Just then her mother's attention was

captured by the spinners and she wandered off to take a look. Juliet suddenly noticed the wood turnery just outside the French windows. Stepping outside again, she stood transfixed as she watched the demonstration. She fingered a small bowl, loving the smooth feel of the wood and admiring the natural light and dark streaks running through it.

'That was fantastic, Steve,' she told the turner as the demonstration came to an end.

Steve grinned broadly. 'Ah, well, I've been doing this for more years than I'd care to remember. I've been to a few craft fayres in my time but this one takes some beating. Pity it's going to be held somewhere else next year.'

'But it's not,' Juliet repeated. This rumour was getting out of hand. 'Let me qualify that Linden Manor Hotel will be hosting it here as usual — of that I'm certain. Whether the other two hotels in the vicinity choose to be involved is another matter entirely.'

Steve stroked his chin. 'Hmm, well, it

may seem like a long way off to you, but we have to work out what we're doing months in advance, you see, and reserve our places.'

Juliet nodded. 'Absolutely, and I can assure you that it'll all be made clear by the time you leave tomorrow evening.'

She caught up with her mother and, after checking that all was well with several more of the stall holders, they went for some refreshments. They were enjoying their coffee and croissants when Marina and her friends came across to their table. Marina knew Alison Croft from the days when Juliet had lodged with her, and before long they were all chattering away like magpies.

Presently, Juliet took the opportunity to take a look at the rest of the stalls in the ballroom. She then positioned herself by the door with a pile of flyers about Linden Manor Hotel and their forthcoming events.

'How's it going?' Scott asked, coming across to join her.

'Good, thanks. There is such an

amazing variety of crafts here — so much talent.' She waited for him to mention the fresh rumours that were being circulated, along with the flyers and, when he didn't, decided that either he wasn't aware of them, or else he'd dismissed them as being nothing to worry about.

She pointed out Marina and her friends, still sitting with her mother, and obviously enjoying a good gossip.

'Oh, perhaps I can snatch a quick break and join them — I'm parched,' Scott said. 'Although I might feel overwhelmed by all those elderly ladies. When everything quietens down next week, perhaps we can have a drink together?'

'Yes, that would be nice, I'll look forward to it,' she told him sincerely.

Left to her own devices, Juliet searched the crowded room for anyone she might recognise. Thankfully, she was aware that the press had visited the previous day. Noticing her uniform, a couple of people stopped to speak to her and introduced themselves as staff from The Grange.

'It must be wonderful to work in a

place like this,' the young woman called Sharon? commented. 'I saw the advert for new staff and, to be honest, I was tempted to apply, but I've only been in my present position for six months.'

'I thought it was everyone's dream to work for Sheldon Enterprises,' Juliet said carefully.

Sharon shrugged. 'Oh, I like it well enough, but it's a bit impersonal. Anyway, it's all good experience, I suppose, and that can't be bad.'

'Sharon doesn't know where she's well off,' her colleague Tony remarked. 'At least our jobs are secure, which is more than a lot of folk can say nowadays.'

Juliet was tempted to sound them out, to find out whether or not they knew anything about a proposed change of venue for the craft fayre, but decided against it. After all, for all she knew, they might be doing the same to her. She hated being so suspicious of everyone.

Eventually they moved off and several visitors stopped to speak to her after that. Much to Juliet's relief, they were all extremely complimentary about the craft fayre.

After Juliet had been standing at her post for about half an hour, Martin appeared at the far end of the ballroom and headed in her direction.

'So there you are! I thought you'd still be outside with your parents.'

'No, my mother's met up with Marina and her friends and my father's spending a lazy morning by the pool; so I've taken the opportunity to do a spot of publicity ... Martin, have you seen this?'

He scanned the flyer Megan had given her in disbelief. 'Who gave it to you?' he demanded.

'Megan.' She told him what she had gleaned and how she'd been tackling the situation.

Martin stared at the piece of paper in his hand as if it were about to explode. 'I don't believe it!' he said at length. 'This flyer is advertising a Christmas Fayre and hotel package that doesn't include us at all.'

Juliet nodded. 'And Megan and Steve

are convinced that the venue is changing for next year because someone has told them that Linden Manor is probably closing. The problem is, we don't know where these rumours are coming from.'

'No, but I intend to find out,' Martin said, his eyes darkening. 'Well done, Juliet for sussing this out! It's my belief that Carl Benfield is behind this. As usual, your common sense and loyalty has prevailed.' He touched her arm briefly, sending a little shiver dancing along her spine at the contact.

Juliet watched as Martin dashed into the foyer, pleased that he valued her input on behalf of the hotel. If only she meant more to him than just a friend and confidante, she thought sadly.

11

The following day, Juliet's parents departed after lunch, having thoroughly enjoyed their stay. She waved them goodbye and returned to reception, knowing that she was going to greatly miss them.

The next hour was so frenetic that she didn't have time to be sad. Admission to the craft fayre was reduced on the last day and, during the afternoon, there was an enormous surge of last minute visitors.

There seemed to be a never-ending stream of enquiries about a variety of different things. Juliet glanced at her watch as Layla went for a very late break.

She had just managed to reunite a tearful, lost child with her equally tearful mother when Mrs Towner appeared in the foyer.

'I've done it!' she informed Juliet triumphantly.

'Sorry, Mrs Towner, I'm afraid you've

lost me — done what?' Juliet enquired, mystified.

'I've discovered who's been planting all those notices Megan's told me about, that's what!' She paused and then added dramatically, '*And* I wouldn't be surprised if she's responsible for starting that rumour about this hotel closing too!'

Juliet's attention was immediately captured. 'Megan? Surely not!'

'Oh, no, not Megan!' Mrs Towner looked horrified.

'So, who is this person then? And how do you know he or she's the culprit?'

Mrs Towner leant over the desk and whispered in a conspiratorial fashion. 'I saw her, didn't I? Could have caught her red-handed, but decided against it. She's a skinny little thing, wearing jeans and a T shirt, dark curly hair.'

Juliet was disappointed. The description could fit just about anyone.

'OK, so what did she actually do, this young girl?'

'She took a pile of flyers from her bag and left them on that lovely candle stall

— right under the very nose of the stall holder who was speaking to a customer at the time — then she darted away.'

There wasn't much to go on, but Juliet thanked Mrs Towner profusely, and ordered her some refreshments on the house.

'What was all that about?' asked Martin, appearing at the desk as soon as Mrs Towner had departed. Juliet explained as best she could.

'Amazing! I've been trying to find out who's behind all this and that little woman has sussed it out for us.'

'So, you obviously know who it is?' Juliet prompted impatiently.

Martin looked cagey. 'Hmm. Let's just say I've got a very strong suspicion, shall we? After speaking with Aunt Jane on the phone last night, everything is slowly beginning to make sense and slot into place. But until I'm absolutely certain of my facts, I'm not prepared to say anything. Thankfully, there's been some very positive feedback about this craft fayre. Did Mrs Towner go into the lounge? I'd like to thank her personally.'

'Yes; I've arranged for her and her husband to have a complimentary cream tea — hope that's OK?'

He grinned. 'On this occasion, yes, but if we make a habit of all these freebies, we'll be giving all the profits away.'

He headed off in the direction of the lounge, and Juliet was relieved that the situation was about to be resolved.

She stood in the doorway with several other members of staff, surveying the scene outside. An admirable job had been made of the cleaning up, and the following morning the groundsmen would move in and restore the grounds to their usual pristine state.

'I'm feeling a bit deflated now this has come to an end. It's been hard work but it was great fun,' Karen said, voicing the thoughts of most of her colleagues.

'There's another one to look forward to at Christmas,' Iain reminded her, slipping an arm about her waist, 'together with a *Turkey and Tinsel* weekend.'

'What's that?' asked Juliet curiously.

'We give the guests all of the Christmas

festivities early. Combined with the Fayre for shopping, it makes for a really lovely experience,' Iain explained.

'It's fun — like having two Christmases,' Layla added. '*And* they have some great evening entertainment.'

But Juliet could see from the expression on Scott's face that he was not impressed. As they moved away from the entrance, he muttered, 'That's just about decided me. All this stuff's not really my scene! I can think of better ways of spending my time … When can we meet up for that drink? I've got something I want to tell you, Juliet.'

'I'm not sure, Scott. Because of my parents visiting, Martin's been very flexible with my work schedule this week, so now I've got to crack on with the refurbishment. It could mean working late in order to catch up.'

Scott scowled. 'D'you know what, Juliet Croft? You're absolutely no fun anymore — no fun at all. You're in great danger of joining Martin and becoming a workaholic!'

And he stormed off towards the lifts, leaving her staring after him open-mouthed at the unfairness of this remark. When she'd simmered down she wondered whatever it was that he wanted to tell her. Perhaps it was important and she'd been a bit uncharitable towards him.

★ ★ ★

Juliet hummed to herself as she put the finishing touches to the chair she'd been re-covering. Standing back, she felt a sense of satisfaction as she surveyed her handiwork.

'Have you seen this?'

Startled she span round to find Martin standing in the doorway brandishing a copy of the local newspaper.

She shook her head and, taking the paper from him, scanned the article about the craft fayre. 'It all seems very positive,' she said, wondering why he was looking so angry.

'Read on. Look at the last paragraph,

on the opposite page,' he urged.

'Oh, I missed that — too busy looking at the photographs.'

She glanced at the paragraph he'd pointed out and gasped as she read: *'There's a rumour circulating amongst the stall-holders that this is the last year the Fayre will be held at Linden Manor Hotel. They understand, from an undisclosed source, that the hotel is experiencing financial difficulties and is likely to be sold in the near future.*

'The assistant manager, Mr Scott Norris, was adamant that this is not the case, but unfortunately, there was no representative from the owners available for comment.'

'This is all we need,' Martin said grimly. 'I was hoping we could manage to sort things out before the press got wind of the situation. I'd no idea they'd already interviewed Scott. He ought to have mentioned it.'

'Have you had a chance to speak with Edwin Benfield?' Juliet asked.

'Not yet. I've left that to Aunt Jane.

261

She doesn't think he's changed his mind about not wanting to sell up, and she certainly hasn't. All this uncertainty is bad for business — it's so unsettling. We don't want any prospective candidates pulling out because they think their jobs will be insecure.'

He looked so forlorn that she wanted to hug him and tell him everything was going to be all right. Instead she merely said, 'It'll work out OK, you'll see, Martin.'

He touched her arm, making her catch her breath. 'Yes, of course it will, especially with guys like you working here. We've got a good team ... I like that chair, by the way — very professional. Your parents were very complimentary about their stay, you know. They loved this room.'

'Yes, they thoroughly enjoyed their visit, *and* they're talking of coming to the *Turkey and Tinsel* weekend. I have to admit I hadn't a clue what it was, but now it's been explained to me, it sounds great fun.'

His face lit up. 'It is. I adore

Christmases here and hope you will too. When I've sorted out some of these problems, perhaps we can get together over a meal and I'll tell you a bit more about it.'

Her heart leapt. She smiled back at him, so aware of his presence beside her. 'Yes please — that would be great!'

He gave her a devastating smile. 'I'll look forward to it. Must dash. I need to catch Scott before he goes off duty.'

A few minutes later Juliet, still on cloud nine, was about to leave the room when Karen rushed in.

'Oh. Good, you are still here. Martin said this is where I'd find you. This room is looking fantastic, Juliet!'

'Thanks — I am quite pleased with the way it's turned out. Just shows what you can do on a shoestring … Karen, why are you waving your hand about? Oh, wow!' she exclaimed, suddenly noticing the ring. 'Congratulations!' She caught hold of her friend's hand and admired the diamond cluster on her engagement finger.

Karen was beaming from ear to ear. 'Thanks. I wanted you to be the first to know, after my family. I've been wearing it round my neck all morning until I could get to see you! We're having an engagement party, just as soon as it can be arranged. Here, if possible, so that people can drift in and out if they're on duty.'

Juliet hugged her friend. 'I'm really happy for you! So, even Martin doesn't know yet?'

'I'm planning to tell him next — and then everyone else. Coming to work here was the best decision I've ever made, but life is so hectic in the office that I can't be spared for more than half an hour.'

'Shoo then, or it'll be time to get back.'

As Juliet watched her friend practically skipping out of the room, she found herself wondering if she would ever experience that kind of happiness.

$\star$ $\star$ $\star$

Juliet got to catch up with Scott and learn his news earlier than expected. Martin offered to do a shift on reception whilst the guests were at dinner that evening so that Karen, Iain and her closest friends could enjoy a celebratory drink in the bar. They arrived to find that Martin had arranged for champagne and plates of canapés to be served.

'Wonderful news about Karen and Iain, isn't it?' Layla said to Juliet, as they made their way towards the table set aside for them.

'Fantastic! Those two are made for one another.'

'I can't get over how generous Martin's been,' Iain remarked as he poured their champagne. 'Karen and I are over-whelmed by people's kindness.'

'That's because the pair of you deserve it,' Layla's boyfriend, Adam, told him.

Shortly afterwards, everyone raised their glasses to the happy couple, and Scott demanded a speech. Blushing wildly, Karen stammered her thanks and mentioned the engagement party which she hoped to arrange for the following weekend. Then the happy couple got to their feet, having arranged to go out for a meal that evening to celebrate.

Scott glanced at his watch. 'We've got about ten minutes before the guests descend on us. I'm on duty in the ballroom tonight — so let's go outside whilst we've got the chance, Juliet, and I can tell you my news.'

Mystified, she followed him out onto the deserted terrace, and they sat on the wall overlooking an expanse of beautifully-kept grass bordered by colourful flowerbeds. In the background, acacia trees contrasted with copper beeches, and the linden trees that gave the manor its name, lined either side of the drive providing a graceful avenue.

'So what's this news you've been bursting to tell me?' she prompted, after a few minutes had elapsed.

'When I was visiting my parents recently, I ran into an old friend I hadn't seen for ages. We got talking and went for a drink. He's just moved back to Herts, and is looking for someone to work with him and help manage the family firm. His father's practically retired due to health problems. So, Dave's asked me if I'd be interested.'

'What about your travel plans?' Juliet asked, taken aback.

'I'd need to get some money together first of all, and that's not going to happen in the immediate future — unless I win the lottery — so I've decided to put it on hold.'

'And what *is* this family firm?' Juliet asked curiously.

'Dave's father is a car salesman. You should see the showroom — very swish. I've always been interested in cars, and I think a complete change is just what I need right now.'

Juliet tried to conceal her doubts and sound positive. 'We-ell, yes, as my old Gran used to say, 'A change is as good as a rest,' and I'm sure she was right.'

Scott nodded. 'I've decided the hotel business is not for me — too insular for my liking. I miss the night life, and the more flexible working hours from when I worked in Herts. Not everyone can be as dedicated to their job as Martin is.'

Scott hesitated and then added,

'Actually, I'm back in touch with Kelly again. Now we've had a period of separation, we've decided to give our relationship another go.'

'I see,' was all Juliet could find to say.

He shot her a surprised glance. 'You're OK with that, aren't you? After all, you've said yourself, we weren't going anywhere. I hope we can remain friends, but you and Martin are far better matched.'

She stared at him, her heart beating rapidly. 'I don't know what you mean, Scott.'

'Oh, I think you do. He's much more on your wavelength than I am. It's obvious he thinks a lot of you, too.'

A slight colour tinged her cheeks. She swallowed. 'As a colleague, perhaps, but had you forgotten he's still involved with Amanda?'

Scott gave her a knowing look. 'Oh, I wouldn't be too sure about that, if I were you. Amanda is a crafty young woman — uses people for her own ends … Anyway, I hope you and I will always remain friends.'

'Absolutely,' she assured him with a smile, wishing she could believe he was right about Martin and Amanda. 'Have you informed Martin you're leaving yet?'

'No, I want to get things finalised first of all. I'm not sure how much notice I'll need to give. You'll keep shtum, won't you?'

'Of course. It'll be difficult to replace you.'

'Sweet of you to say so, but Iain's shaping up well. I'm sure he could be persuaded to step into my shoes — even if it's only in a temporary capacity. Marriage is an expensive business, so I expect he'll need to save every penny he can get.'

'I'm going to miss you,' she told him sincerely.

'And I'll miss you too.' He slung an arm about Juliet's waist and gave her a hug.

They were unaware that Martin, who had finished his stint on reception, was standing by the open doorway. He sighed as he watched the two of them chatting intimately together. Painful as it was, he knew that he was going to have to accept that Juliet and Scott were becoming very close. He took his mobile from his pocket and dialled Amanda's number. It was high time they had a heart to heart, and he wasn't looking forward to it …

Juliet was about to join some of her colleagues for a very late dinner when she practically bumped into Amanda, who was hovering in the foyer looking a million dollars in a short red dress that emphasised her curvaceous figure and wonderful tan.

'Have you seen Martin anywhere?' she demanded, flicking back her blonde hair.

'I think he's in the lounge talking to some of the guests. Do you want me to tell him you're here?'

'No, I'll find him.' A little smile curved her lips as she informed Juliet, 'He's booked a table at the Country Club, and we'll be late if he doesn't hurry up. He's such a glutton for work, isn't he? But I'm going to make sure he relaxes this evening … Bye.'

Juliet had suddenly lost her appetite.

Scott was so wrong. It was apparent that Martin and Amanda were still very much together. How could she have been foolish enough to have imagined otherwise, she asked herself miserably. She went into the dining-room and made pretence of eating, hoping no-one would notice how quiet she was.

'Did you see the article in the local paper about the Fayre?' one of the waiters asked those nearest him.

'Certainly did! It's a pity they've got hold of that ridiculous rumour, isn't it?' one of his friends replied.

'I hope it really is a rumour and there's no truth in it. Some of the kitchen staff are getting a bit edgy, wondering if their jobs are safe,' Layla's fiancé, Adam, commented.

'Kirsty was telling me a friend of hers was all set to come here for an interview next week, but has decided against it. She's applying for a job at The Grange instead. What do you think, Juliet?' one of the office staff asked her.

'Me?' Juliet came to with a start,

realising that her colleagues were looking at her expectantly. 'Oh, I, er, suppose we should trust in the management and not waste time speculating,' she replied, trying to be diplomatic.

'You would say that,' one of the waitresses told her. 'After all, you and Martin Glover are as thick as thieves, aren't you? But those of us with children and mortgages *do* have to worry about whether our jobs are on the line.'

Several of the others nodded agreement, and Juliet desperately wished Martin was there to back her up in a difficult situation. Deep down, she sympathised with them, but there was little she could say at present to pacify them.

She declined dessert and went off for a walk to clear her head. Perhaps Scott was the sensible one in making the decision to move on.

* * *

On Sunday, Juliet had a free afternoon and, for once, she couldn't wait to get away from Linden Manor. When she'd rung Marina on Friday she'd promptly invited Juliet to Sunday lunch.

'I'll do something that won't spoil if you're a bit late, and we can have a good chinwag. Do you suppose Scott is free?'

'Actually, he's got a day off tomorrow and I know he's going to Herts, so he'll be back on duty again on Sunday.'

'Oh, that's a pity. There's nothing wrong, is there? In Herts, I mean. Only I know he only went there recently. Are the family well?'

'Yes, as far as I'm aware,' Juliet had said carefully. It was not up to her to tell Marina of Scott's plans, or that he was back with Kelly. She hoped he'd do that himself before too long but, before then, he was going to have to speak with Martin.

After a wonderful Sunday lunch, Juliet took Marina for a country drive. There was a garden open to the public as part of the National Gardens Scheme that the older lady particularly wanted to see. It was attractive, colourful and beautifully maintained but not overly large, so it didn't take too long to walk round it.

As Juliet stooped to sniff a fragrant shrub, she remembered the occasions when she had been in the staff garden with Martin, and wished he were here now.

'Let's have a sit down and a cup of tea, and then we can go round again,' Marina suggested. 'I'd like to take another look at the roses; it was getting a bit crowded just now.'

They were sitting on the patio enjoying tea and slices of homemade cake, when a familiar voice asked, 'Mind if I join you?'

Juliet didn't need to look up to realise it was Martin grinning down at them, as he balanced a plate with an enormous slice of chocolate cake and a cup of tea. Her heart missed a beat.

'Martin, whatever are you doing here?' Marina exclaimed in surprise.

He chuckled at the astonished expressions on their faces. 'Same as you, I expect.'

He perched on a rather small plastic

garden chair. 'Actually, Aunt Jane told me about this garden. It belongs to the daughter and son-in-law of friends of hers. I thought I'd come and take a look so I could tell her all about it. Wonderful, isn't it?'

Bemused, Juliet nodded. She'd been thinking about Martin and now, here he was, just as if she'd conjured him up out of thin air!

Marina wiped a crumb from her mouth. 'That coffee and walnut cake was delicious ... I always hope to pick up gardening tips from these events. We're going to take another look at the roses.'

'Yes, they're magnificent, aren't they? Apparently, there's a flower festival on at the local church this weekend too. The lady of the house has made an arrangement, so I said I'd take a look. Would you be interested in joining me?'

Marina smiled her delight. 'I love flower festivals, but won't it be over by now?'

He shook his head. 'Apparently, there's a short service to round it all off at six o'clock. Can you stay until then?'

Juliet, very much wanting to say *yes*, looked at Marina, who was probably planning to go to the evening service at her own church.

Marina smiled at Martin. 'That would be lovely. I saw the poster and gather there's a choir from the local school singing especially for the occasion.'

After they'd taken another look at the roses, Juliet and Martin waited patiently whilst Marina purchased some plants.

'Scott told me his news today,' Martin said conversationally. 'I gather you know already. Are you planning to join him in Hertfordshire?'

'Join him in a car sales-room? No way!' Juliet exclaimed, horrified that Martin could think such a thing.

He laughed. 'That's a relief, but I didn't actually mean that.'

'So, what did you mean, Martin?' she asked, head on one side.

The colour tinged his cheeks. 'I assumed — that is I thought you and Scott ...'

Marina, having made her purchases was coming towards them along the path, looking pleased with herself.

Juliet said hastily, 'Don't say anything about this to Marina. Scott hasn't spoken to her yet. I'd no idea things had progressed so quickly.' She took a deep breath. 'Martin — I just want you to know, there is absolutely nothing going on between myself and Scott. We're just good friends. You must believe me.'

Martin had no chance to reply because, just then, Marina joined them slightly out of breath. 'Goodness, I don't know where I'm going to put all these plants but I simply couldn't resist them … So, where's this church, Martin? I'm dying to take a look. I don't know this area very well, and can't remember seeing it when we arrived.'

'I think it's hidden away behind that clump of trees. Look, you can just see the spire! Come on, let's go and find it.'

The flower festival in the fourteenth century church was spectacular. Juliet was admiring an eye-catching display of flowers, when Martin took her elbow and pointed to Marina who stood transfixed in front of a particularly colourful arrangement by the font.

'She's really enjoying this, isn't she?' he whispered.

'Certainly is — it was a good idea of yours to suggest we came here.'

But then Martin was that sort of person, she reflected, kind and considerate.

'I've enjoyed it too. It'll be something else to tell Aunt Jane, and it's given us some more time together,' he said quietly. 'I'm glad you've told me about you and Scott. For one awful moment, I thought you'd decided to return to Herts with him.'

'Are you telling me you would have minded if I had?' she asked softly.

His green eyes searched her face. 'You know I would. I've come to care about you, Juliet, and I had hoped that ...'

A hush descended on the church signalling the beginning of the short service, and everyone settled in the pews. The children's choir was a delight and everyone applauded loudly as the singing came to an end.

The rest of the service was simple but meaningful. During the final hymn, *All Things Bright and Beautiful*, obviously chosen for the children's benefit, Juliet was very aware of Martin sitting beside her singing in his baritone voice. She remembered the occasion of the talent contest and knew that she wanted to be beside this man for the rest of her life.

Marina, on Juliet's other side, stole a glance at them and smiled to herself. She had a strong feeling things were going in the right direction for the pair of them at long last.

'That was most enjoyable,' Martin remarked as they walked back towards the field where their cars were parked.

'It certainly was. You'd be very welcome to come back with us and have some supper,' Marina invited.

'Much as I'd love too, regretfully, I've got to be back at Linden Manor by eight o'clock,' he told her.

'Why, what happens if you don't? Do

you turn into a frog?' Marina enquired wittily.

'That's an interesting thought. I'd have to hope that a princess would come along and kiss me and turn me back into a human again,' he said, and briefly his eyes met Juliet's.

12

'Good morning. Could you tell me where I can find Martin Glover?'

Looking up, Juliet saw a distinguished-looking man with a shock of white hair and bright blue eyes standing in front of the reception desk. 'Tell him Edwin Benfield is here, will you my dear?' he added.

Even before he had given his name, Juliet had guessed who he was.

'Certainly, Mr Benfield, I'll find him for you,' she replied, wondering if Martin was expecting him. She rang Martin's mobile and, shortly, Karen appeared to take the elderly gentleman to his office. The two women managed to exchange a quick, meaningful glance.

After an hour or so Karen reappeared. 'Martin's asked if you can be spared to show Mr Benfield the refurbishments. Apparently, he'd like to have a word with you, personally … It's OK, Juliet, he's not a bit like his son, so you can relax for the moment! I gather Carl Benfield will be making an appearance around lunch time.'

'Why d'you think he's here?' asked Layla anxiously. 'Is it bad news?'

'Now you know I'm not able to divulge anything confidential, although I can tell you that both the Benfields will be staying on for the interviews this afternoon.'

Layla pulled a face. 'Rather those poor candidates than me. Take as long as you need, Juliet, then you can cover for me so I can take my lunch break with Adam.'

A few minutes later Juliet joined Martin and Edwin Benfield, and they took the lift to the third floor.

'Martin and my sister have been explaining what you've been doing, Juliet. It all sounds most enterprising,' Edwin Benfield told her. 'I'm keen to take a look for myself. Just as long as you don't get too carried away, my dear. Unfortunately, there's no bottomless purse.'

Juliet endeavoured not to look in

Martin's direction. 'No, I realise that, but the staff bed-sitters truly did need a face lift.'

First of all, Martin unlocked the door of the room Juliet was just about to begin refurbishing, so that Edwin Benfield would be able to see the contrast.

The elderly gentleman gave a short whistle. 'My goodness, this is in a bad way! It's such a long time since I was here, so I can only remember it as it used to be way back.'

'Was it the servants' quarters up here?' Juliet asked, her face alight with interest.

'No, my dear, there's another floor above this one and, years back, that was their domain. These were additional guest rooms but, as time went on, they weren't needed. I seem to remember my sister, Jane, chose to sleep up here at one time … We certainly can't expect the staff to sleep in conditions like this! You ought to have told me, Martin.'

Martin looked taken aback. 'I have discussed it with Carl several times. I got the distinct impression that you, er, weren't interested in further refurbishment.'

Edwin stroked his chin. 'Did you indeed? I have to admit I've left most of the decision-making to Carl recently. We'll all need to have a proper discussion this afternoon — after those interviews.'

'Would you like to see the staff bedsitter we've just finished doing up?' Juliet asked, to fill an awkward pause. She led the way along the corridor and they paused briefly to inspect the bathroom.

Edwin Benfield's bushy eyebrows rose as he looked at the newly-refurbished staff quarters. 'My goodness! What a transformation! This is more like it. And you're responsible for this work, young lady?'

Juliet coloured. 'Oh, I'm afraid I can't take all the credit. I came up with several ideas, and re-covered those armchairs but apart from that, several people have lent a hand, including Martin.'

Juliet hoped fervently that Edwin Benfield approved. She stood with her fingers crossed behind her back, aware that so much rested on the older man's approval. Whatever happened, she didn't want to let Martin down.

There was a silence and then Edwin said, 'I certainly wouldn't mind sleeping in this room myself. Well done, my dear! I would just ask you one thing ...' Edwin paused.

Juliet felt apprehensive as she wondered what he was about to say.

He cleared his throat. 'I can't help wondering what you're all hoping to achieve. I mean, why would you do all this, when you don't know if my sister and I are going to rub our hands in glee and sell this place anyway?'

'We, er — we just hoped you'd change your mind when you could see how keen we were to put Linden Manor Hotel on the map,' she ventured, not daring to look at Martin.

'Oh, so it wouldn't have anything to do with the fact that I've got the reputation for being a tight-fisted old codger, who wouldn't open the coffers for anyone then?' he asked, winking at her.

Juliet flushed scarlet and Martin asked,

'Now, what on earth makes you say that?'

Edwin Benfield chuckled. 'Because, according to my sister, it's what everyone else is saying. She gave me quite an ear-bashing — which was partly why I decided it was high time I came here to take a look at what was going on for myself ... Who made those wonderful curtains?'

'We've employed a lady called Marina Norris, who used to work at Cramphorn's. Actually, she's our assistant manager's aunt.'

'Marina Norris,' Edwin mused. 'There used to be a Marina Norris who lived round here many moons ago — used to go out with my brother, Miles.'

'That's the same lady,' Juliet told him.

His eyes widened. 'Well, well! Life's full of surprises. And you say Scott Norris is her nephew, Martin?'

'Yes, but as I've told you he's moving on shortly.'

'You don't seem to have much luck with your assistant managers, Martin,' Edwin commented drily. 'And what's this

I hear about Amanda Pearson moving to America?'

Martin's face was an absolute picture. 'America! That's the first I've heard of it. Who told you that?'

Edwin Benfield tapped his nose. 'I have my sources, my boy. She's a very ambitious young woman, that one. Going to be working for the American branch of Sheldon Enterprises.'

There was a silence and then Juliet said brightly, 'Would you like to see the newly-refurbished guest room, Mr Benfield?'

'Yes, indeed. Lead on.'

As they took the lift to the floor below, Juliet stole a glance at Martin who looked as though he was in a daze. She wondered what had made Amanda suddenly decide to go to America, and why she hadn't confided in Martin.

'This is amazing,' Edwin Benfield said, surveying the newly decorated guest room. 'And you obviously think we can justify the expense of doing it up?'

'Absolutely,' Martin said. 'Besides, it hasn't cost a fraction of what Sheldon

Interiors would have charged three years back.'

Edwin Benfield gave Juliet an approving look. 'Well, you're certainly earning your keep, young woman! My sister tells me two of the additional staff will be sleeping in these rooms until more of the staff bed-sitting rooms are redecorated. We'll have to make sure they don't get too used to a life of luxury.'

'They won't,' Martin assured him. 'They're actually going to have a couple of rooms back along the corridor that are still waiting to be done up. Now, if you've seen all that you need to for the time being, shall we have some lunch?'

The elderly gentleman beamed. 'Thought you'd never ask! Breakfast was hours ago, and only continental.'

Juliet declined the invitation to join them for lunch and returned to the desk, much to the relief of Layla who was champing at the bit wanting to take her own break with Adam. Juliet decided to keep quiet about what she'd just heard concerning Amanda.

'Carl Benfield arrived a few minutes ago,' Layla informed her as she collected her bag from beneath the desk. 'He's in the dining-room waiting for his father and Martin.'

'Phew, I'm glad I didn't join them for lunch then. Edwin Benfield just invited me.'

Layla's eyes widened. 'Goodness, you must have impressed him. He obviously liked the décor in the new rooms, then?'

Juliet shrugged. 'He seemed to, but who can tell? Anyway, I don't think they'd be interviewing for new members of staff if they were planning to close us down, do you?'

'Who knows?' Layla spread her hands and went off to join Adam, who was pointedly studying the lunch menu.

The interviews were to be held from two o'clock onwards. Several of the candidates had already arrived in reception, so Juliet directed them to the small lounge where they were to wait. She remembered the previous time when there had been interviews on the day of the Homes and Gardens Fayre, and smiled to herself. It all seemed such an age ago. Such a lot had happened since then.

'Hi, remember me?' Looking up, Juliet saw Sharon, the young woman from The Grange, smiling at her.

'Yes, of course I do. So have you decided to apply for a job here after all?'

'Certainly have. You all seemed such a nice crowd when I came to the craft fayre, so I thought I'd give it a go.'

'Best of luck. This is a nice place to work ... you need to wait in the small lounge, just through there.'

Juliet found it hard to concentrate that afternoon. She was determined not to get too elated at the prospect of Amanda Pearson going off to America. Perhaps Edwin Benfield had got it wrong. But suddenly, she had a good feeling about things in general.

Scott came into reception bursting with news. 'You'll never believe what I've just heard on the grapevine.'

'Go on, surprise me.' Juliet continued to check a booking on the computer screen.

'Amanda's going to America to work for Sheldon Enterprises.'

'Yes, I've heard that too,' she said, and looking up, saw his astonished expression.

'Why am I always the last to get to hear anything round here?' he complained.

'Edwin Benfield happened to mention it — even Martin didn't know. What about you?'

'The same. I was summoned to take coffee with the Powers That Be, after they'd had their lunch. Martin had to go off to check that everything was ready for the interviews, and they subjected me to a grilling about why I was leaving — said it would help them when looking for future candidates ... You needn't look like that, Juliet! I honestly didn't say a word out of place. Actually, they asked if I'd consider becoming Events Manager specifically for this hotel, instead of what I'm doing now'

'Really? So did you accept?'

'No. I'd already explained my reasons for leaving, and they seemed to accept that. So I thanked them nicely and said I was now committed to my new job in

Hertfordshire. It felt good to be asked, though. It appears they want to break their ties with the other hotels from now on, do their own thing.'

'Wow! That's going to upset the apple-cart!' Juliet exclaimed, trying to absorb all this.

Scott grinned. 'Isn't it just! Carl Benfield didn't say too much — left it all to his father, which was surprising. To my mind, he seemed a tad subdued, so it'll be interesting to see what transpires. I've got a strong feeling he's not going to be getting so much of his own way in future.'

⋆ ⋆ ⋆

It was much later in the day, after the interviews were over and the Benfields had departed, that Martin appeared in reception looking punch-drunk.

'I have never needed a break as much as I need one now,' he told Juliet with a wry grin. 'When are you off duty? D'you fancy getting away for a couple of hours or so?'

Juliet's heart leapt. 'Seven o'clock and that would be fantastic ... walking or what?'

'Have you eaten?' She shook her head. 'Then how about a country drive and a pub meal?' he suggested.

They arranged to meet at seven-thirty, which just gave Juliet sufficient time to take a quick shower, change into a pair of white trousers and a sky-blue tunic top and apply some light make-up.

Martin was waiting for her on the terrace, gazing out across the grounds. She stood by his side, catching the clean, fresh scent of his cologne. He'd changed too, into smart jeans and a dark-blue shirt.

He turned to smile at her. 'I never tire of this view. I find it relaxing to come out here at the end of a stressful day.'

'Mmm. It is lovely and certainly has a calming effect.'

He slipped an arm through hers. 'I thought we'd turn left at the bottom of the drive — go past the cottage where my grandparents used to live and out into the heart of the country. We can stop at the first pub we come to that serves food.'

'What a lovely idea — sounds like a mystery tour.'

'It'll be that all right. I haven't a clue where we'll end up!' He grinned at her. 'Sure you trust me not to lose the pair of us?'

'Absolutely,' she assured him, eyes shining, knowing that she would feel safe with Martin whatever the circumstances.

It was another lovely evening and, as they drove along narrow lanes with spectacular views across fields ready for harvesting, Juliet sighed with pure contentment. 'This part of Kent is so beautiful,' she said, as he shot her a questioning glance. 'So did you manage to appoint any of the candidates?'

'Oh yes, a couple were very suitable. You've probably met one of them — works at The Grange but finds it a bit too large and impersonal.'

'Oh, Sharon Slade? I'm glad you've appointed her. She seems such a nice person.'

'Mmm. That's what we thought. Her

CV is impressive too. We're going to need another round of interviews to appoint a third member of staff, which is what Edwin Benfield thinks is appropriate. We'll then need to think about advertising Scott's post. That means deciding if we need a separate Events Manager. Has Scott had the opportunity to mention this to you?'

'Actually, yes. He was made up to be asked, but hasn't changed his mind about returning to Herts. Do I take it you're not going to be so involved with the other two hotels?'

Martin swerved to avoid a rabbit. 'Seems like it, but that's obviously down to Edwin and Aunt Jane. Look, I know this won't go any further, but I really need to tell someone ...'

'Then I'm flattered you've chosen me. If it's to do with Amanda, then I'm sorry she didn't tell you about America herself. It must have been quite a shock to find out the way that you did.'

He nodded. There was a pause and then he said, 'Amanda is an extremely restless young woman. Scott is the male counterpart. I thought she was probably looking for promotion within Sheldon Enterprises, but I'd no idea she was thinking of going abroad.'

'I expect you'll miss her,' Juliet said quietly, watching for his reaction.

His hands tightened slightly on the wheel. 'Oh, I think we miss all our colleagues when they move on. But no matter what you might have thought, Juliet, Amanda and I have never been that close. She can be a bit manipulative if she wants to get her own way.'

There was a silence as Juliet mulled over what Martin had just told her. She stole another look at him, but his face was expressionless as he concentrated on the narrow lane in front of him.

She swallowed. 'But she asked you out to Spain,' she pointed out.

Martin gave a little laugh. 'She was trying to make Jamie jealous. It didn't work because he already has a girlfriend — Carl Benfield's daughter, Chloe. Our mischievous young person who left all those flyers on the stalls last week.'

Juliet's attention was diverted away from Amanda. 'I don't understand ... Why would this Chloe do such a thing?'

'Oh, I can answer that. I'll tell you when we're sitting comfortably over a meal. It's all tied up with what I really wanted to talk to you about.'

Suddenly as they rounded a bend the lane widened out, and there in front of them was a picturesque, white-washed pub with a quantity of colourful hanging baskets.

'Let's hope they're still doing food. It's gone eight o'clock and I'm famished. Lunch was hours ago.'

Juliet hoped they were too, as her stomach was beginning to feel empty. Fortunately, meals were still being served. They opted to stay inside, admiring the oak beams and ancient red-brick fireplace with the rows of horse-brasses hanging on either side. They sat enjoying a drink whilst their meal was being cooked.

'What's the story about Carl Benfield's

daughter?' Juliet asked, setting down her glass.

'Yes, let's get that out of the way first. Carl Benfield was so convinced his father and Aunt Jane were prepared to sell Linden Manor that he'd been sounding out prospective buyers like Sheldon Enterprises, and getting to know the set-up.'

Juliet frowned. 'But I don't understand. How exactly would the sale have been of benefit to Carl?'

Martin cupped his chin in his hands. 'I can only assume that he thought he'd be able to persuade Edwin to give him part of his inheritance early. As we know, Carl's lost interest in Linden Manor. Apparently, he's got several ventures he's keen to invest in. I've heard most of this from Aunt Jane.'

Juliet nodded. 'So when he realised it was a no go area and his father and Jane didn't want to sell Linden Manor after all, he got Chloe to try and muddy the hotel's name so they might change their minds.'

'Got it in one! By this time, Carl had become very pally with the manager at Sheldon's and Chloe had met Jamie at a party. To my mind, Sheldon's have never been above a bit of dirty dealing, so it's anyone's guess who started those rumours and where the flyers came from.

'It's my belief we're never likely to find out for sure. It seems Chloe hoped that when Amanda left, she'd get her job. That's probably why Amanda and Jamie were dining with Carl that evening, so that Carl could test the water for Chloe and find out about a few other things.'

Juliet clicked her fingers. 'But when Sheldon's realised Edwin Benfield wasn't going to budge they made the decision that if they couldn't have Linden Manor Hotel as part of their group, then they weren't interested in joining in with our events anymore.'

He nodded. 'Absolutely correct! But, you see, Aunt Jane and Edwin weren't that concerned. They thought it was high time we broke away and went it alone …'

Martin trailed off as their food arrived.

As they tucked into steak, salad and chips their conversation turned to other things. They discussed holidays they'd taken, their tastes in music and films, and generally got to know one another.

Over coffee, as they got on to the topic of the theatre, Martin said, 'There's a theatre group that travels round doing open-air productions so I thought we might hire them next year.'

'What a brilliant idea! So you're convinced that we'll all still have a job by then?' she teased.

There was a mysterious expression on Martin's face. 'Ah well, I still haven't shared my news with you. I've kept the very best piece till last! I've known it might happen for a long while now, but it's difficult for me to believe that anyone could be so generous.'

He paused for so long that Juliet was forced to prompt him. 'Come on, don't keep me in suspense,' she pleaded.

'Aunt Jane has decided to give me a part share in the hotel. She said I might as well have it now rather than later, when she's, er, gone.'

'Wow that's fantastic!' Juliet gasped. 'She's such a lovely lady, and she obviously thinks the world of you.'

Martin nodded, and she could see that he was quite emotional. She stretched out her hand and placed it over his. 'Aunt Jane's been like a mother to me these past years,' he said gruffly. 'And that's not all. Edwin and Jane have a cousin, Mark, who's very much younger than them, and keen to invest in the hotel. Edwin is prepared to sell him part of his share. If Mark decides to go ahead, then the capital that Edwin raises can go to Carl.'

'Carl doesn't deserve it,' she told him. 'So, will this Mark do Carl's job?'

'For the time being, yes. He's always loved Linden Manor and him and his family are prepared to move to Kent. Apparently, Carl's always fobbed him off when he's shown too much of an interest in the place.'

'Protecting his own interests, I suspect. So — just to get everything clear in my mind — has Chloe got the job she was hankering after?'

He shook his head. 'She's not nearly experienced enough, but she *is* going to work at The Grange so she can prove her worth — and see more of Jamie, of course.'

'What a story! And is that really everything?'

He squeezed her hand gently. 'No, I don't think it ends quite there, Juliet.'

Her lovely hazel eyes widened. 'What more could there possibly be?'

'There's our own story,' he said quietly. 'Come on, it's time to go home. I'll finish it on the way.'

Bemused, Juliet wondered whatever he meant. As they began the drive back to Linden Manor he said, 'Did you know we share some history where the Sheldons are concerned?'

Juliet was mystified. 'I'm afraid you've lost me, Martin. You're going to have to explain.'

'I've known for a long time that you used to go out with Evan Dean.'

Juliet gasped. This was the last thing

she'd expected him to say! 'How did you find out?'

'Because, before he came on the scene, I happened to be engaged to Elizabeth Sheldon ... Say something!' he implored at last, as the silence lengthened.

'You've rendered me speechless,' she managed at last. 'I'd absolutely no idea.'

'I've put that episode behind me now but, for a long time, I buried myself in my work at Linden Manor. And then, when I discovered you were the woman Evan had let down, it seemed as if we were destined to be brought together.'

'My old gran used to say that everything happens for a purpose,' she said softly, her heart hammering.

'Your old gran was obviously very wise.' He pulled into a convenient passing place. 'And there's been so much misunderstanding because of Scott and Amanda but, hopefully, we've sorted all that out now.'

'Yes,' she whispered. 'So can we move on to the next part of the story, please?'

'I'd like that very much,' he told her

and caught her in his arms. He traced the outline of her face, caressed her tenderly, and then his lips met hers. Filled with ecstasy she reached up and entwined her fingers in his thick hair. She felt the warmth emanating from him, was aware of the magnetism between them. His kisses set her very being on fire, and she knew that this was where she belonged — in the shelter of his arms.

★　★　★

Karen's engagement party was going with a swing. After the happy couple and their family and friends had enjoyed an elaborate buffet, provided by Chef and his team, everyone went into the ballroom where the hotel guests were invited to join in the dancing.

It was a happy, sparkling occasion. Most of the staff managed to join in at some point during the evening.

'I love working here,' Karen told Juliet, breathless from the last dance. 'It's just like belonging to one big, happy family.'

Juliet nodded as she looked towards

the door watching for any sign of Martin. He'd breezed in and out of the dining-room about an hour ago, but she hadn't set eyes on him since. It was almost ten o'clock when he finally put in an appearance. Her heart seemed to miss a beat at the sight of him. He came straight across to her.

'Edwin rang up for a long chat,' he told her with a smile that accentuated the dimple in his chin. 'It was very worthwhile. Mark's definitely going to invest in this hotel. Isn't that wonderful news?'

'It certainly is. What a relief! When are you going to tell the others?'

'All in good time. When things are settled. Come on, let's dance.'

He held out his hand to her as the music struck up again. It was the first time she'd danced with him, and they matched each other's steps perfectly. 'You're looking absolutely lovely tonight,' he murmured against her hair. 'I love that blue dress and the way you've done your hair.'

She smiled at him, and it was as if they

were in an enchanted world of their own.

'I'm afraid I don't go in for big, extravagant gestures,' he said, a little smile playing about his lips, 'so, if I asked you to marry me, would you settle for a quiet sort of wedding, with the service in the local church, the reception in a marquee on the lawn out there — and most of the people here as guests?'

'That would suit me just fine, Mr Glover,' she breathed, eyes sparkling with joy. As his lips met hers, Juliet knew she had found the man of her dreams at last.